"Don't think about what can happen in a month. Don't think about what can happen in a year. Just focus on the 24 hours in front of you and do what you can to get closer to where you want to be!"
Eric Thomas

"Don't make a habit out of choosing what feels good over what's actually good for you."
Eric Thomas

"Your relationships will either make you or break you, and there is no such thing as a neutral relationship. People either inspire you to greatness or pull you down in the gutter, it's that simple. No one fails alone, and no one succeeds alone."
Eric Thomas

SHADOWS UNDER A DIPPING SUN

Copyright © 2024 By R.P. Falconer
Published by Silverstone Publishing

For Harlesden, my home. For London, my city, and all of her children.

To Acala & Nia. May God continue
to bless you both.

Shadows under a dipping sun.

An old, rusty train rolled slowly past a children's park located below a grassy verge; its wheels groaned with age and the burden of cargo shackled to its iron hind.

The train always seized Paul's attention, this magnificent hulk managing to crawl by in relative silence - used to transport the world's wares to London and beyond - breaking beams of street light on the other side of the tracks, where Irish travellers lived when they felt like it.

Paul always wondered where it came from and where it would go. Whether along its route, young people with better prospects than theirs stood at attention, observing its inevitable arrival and departure, sparing thoughts for less fortunate children. He doubted it, though; lessons in his short life span had taught him that people tended to always think up rather than down.

Apparently, he lived in a deprived area, but to him and most, 'Church End' was simply home.

A collection of medium-sized, white plastic and orange brick blocks that packed in all its residents and their myriad of socio-economic issues, human eyesores, deliberately kept out of the way of what seemed like the real world heading 'West'.

"You're always watching that train..." Rich said, pulling his roll-up back to life, its small burning head orange against the darkness of night.

"Do you ever think about where it goes?" Paul questioned.

Rich looked thoughtful.

"It's a freight train; it goes everywhere," Rich replied.

Paul remained silent, observing the final carriage of the train disappear into the distance and darkness, its red tail lights, like the eyes of a demon, in slithering retreat.

"One day, I'll find out..." Paul whispered.

Rich raised his eyebrows and gave the notion a nod.

He took one final drag of his roll-up, then crushed it into a small ball and flicked it over the fencing towards the train track.

He exhaled a large cloud of smoke - drifting away until it expired.

The two walked home together.

A group of older teenagers (C10 gang) had gathered on the corner by an old orphanage situated in the middle of a fork in the road, which divided the route from the park, creating two paths to the front and rear sides of their housing estate.

"Yo! Eediot bwoys," Leon shouted at Paul and Rich as they passed.

Leon's comment evoked laughter from his gang.

Rich and Paul kept their heads down and continued on.

"Oi!" another barked. "Oi, look, look!".

"I really hate these guys," Paul whispered between him and Rich.

Rich looked over at Leon, who stood out from his friends, wielding a serrated-edged knife as long as his thigh.

Leon grinned, making several slashing motions through the air before pushing the knife back into his tracksuit bottom's waistband.

Rich turned away, his face in an unsettled grimace.

Paul and Rich proceeded in silence for a minute until they were beyond the gang's sight.

Approaching Rich's block of flats, they slowed to a stop.

"What was it?" Paul asked Rich, referring to what Leon had shown.

Rich didn't respond.

"Rich…are you cool? You've been acting weird tonight." Paul continued.

Rich looked like a fifteen-year-old boy burdened with stress beyond his years. He drew a deep breath and exhaled.

"My mum's thinking of moving me to my dad's," Rich replied.

"Your mum's what…?" Paul responded, his brow furrowed, his eyes squinting as if he were trying to see a physical manifestation of his friend's astonishing words.

"Yeah, bro… She's worried about me round here," Rich replied, moving his finger about in an irregular circle.

Paul stood on the kerb in complete disbelief; his world, raised to decay by nine words and Rich's mother.

What he ought to have regarded as positive progression for a friend amounted to nothing more than a self-centred sentiment of misplaced abandonment.

However, worse still, it highlighted the dire lack of Paul's future prospects.

Paul didn't have a fancy dad retreat, or anywhere else in the world to go beyond the brick and plastic housing blocks which carved out his perimeter.

Regrettably, this was to be a reality that Paul would now face unaccompanied by one of the few people who understood him most.

Josephine

Mr Briefcase's fall from grace had been much more rapid than the rest of the addicts Josephine was keeping track of.

His once well-tailored suit was now baggy, and his shoes had long lost their lustre. Without a good belt, his heels walked on the backs of his trousers, creating holes where they rubbed.

Leaning and unlaced. His once exquisite footwear had deteriorated due to excessive use, ultimately being rescued from total ruin by the exceptional craftsmanship of the designer label from whence they originated.

She knew he had been a man of wealth because she had overheard him, when he was still healthy, telling his drug dealers that his shoes cost more than three months of their mother's rent, before speeding off in his red sports car - this was a mere thirteen months ago, long before he had begun to erase himself; his transformation from a banker getting a bit of cocaine at the weekend to a shambling addict was remarkable; he no longer belonged to himself, but to the sickly sweet-smelling rock those boys on the corner kept on their person.

Strangely, Mr Briefcase still carried his briefcase to pick up and pay; the filthy, ill-gotten tender would emerge from it and into the hands of the drug dealers.

In return, he would fill the case with whatever drugs he could afford.

Josephine wished to believe that, somehow, from under the drug's vice-like grip, his humanity could be reclaimed - that his briefcase served as a personal reminder that, at some point, he needed to return to his former life, wife and children.

The drug addicts fascinated her the most about where she lived. In her mind, they were the only people seen as worse off than her or the rest of the residents in the area.

Over the last two years, she had observed the drug addicts toiling tirelessly under the scorching sun, snow, rain and wind, their addiction paramount, risking their lives and limbs for drugs.

Some of the items they bartered when funds were limited included stolen televisions, joints of meat, perfumes in shopping trolleys, and offers of themselves.

She had never witnessed or heard the boys below accept the latter, which made them feel somewhat more humane than most would grant.

For over a year, she had begun to keep notes of the drug dealers and users in her diary.

Her vantage point was perfect; her mother's flat overlooked the park and orphanage where the drug dealers would congregate outside to peddle their crud.

In addition to seeing, she would hear each of their words as clear as crystal.

What began as a bit of amusement by giving the drug users names evolved into a comprehensive study, noting their rate of deterioration and chronicling their ever-changing behaviours.

She found her subjects' conduct at the beginning of their addiction was always varied, given that the decay hadn't fully set in - their personalities were still personal.

Still, once their time on the pipe had become prolonged, they all began to behave like one homogeneous entity, shuffling zombie-like humans hell-bent on getting high.

Like Mr Briefcase, very few held out for long, but all believed they were in control of their situation when, in reality, they were attempting to hold water in a sieve, unaware they were slowly softening the wooden floor beneath their feet.

Feeling tired, Josephine shut her diary and slid it to one side on her tiny desk. She turned on her table lamp, stood up, walked to the light switch on the wall by her door, and switched the room light off.

She went to her bed and sat on its edge, listening to the gang below mocking the boys who smoked in the park.

"Yo! Eediot bwoys", she heard her brother's friend Leon scream, the same brother who would come into her room in the early hours and kiss her crown when he thought she was asleep and whisper "Love you, sis."

She pondered how someone so compassionate could be so cruel, and contemplated which part of their shared childhood he had acquired this blot of wickedness, that appeared to run throughout him and his cohorts.

One day, he would never come into her room again - the thought played over in her head like a skipping record and squeezed tears from her face.

The idea felt unfair, but it seemed inevitable given her brother's record and that of the many who had walked that ill-advised path before him.

Herbert

Bay-rum fell in a fine mist over Leon, forcing him forward in a pain-induced "hiss", one eye in a trembling wink as if he had wind that would not pass. The barber offered more antiseptic spray for his freshly cut head, but Leon waved him off, his expensive gold chaps and chain jingling.

Leon stood up from the chair.

The barber removed the apron pinned around his throat and dusted the back of his neck with a brush.

Once the barber had finished, Leon picked up a mirror hung on a small hook to his right and checked the back of his head.

Satisfied, he withdrew a large roll of pink, purple and blue banknotes from his jeans pocket and gave the barber his fee.

Leon walked over to the customers' waiting area, sat beside Paul, and began adjusting and brushing hair from his clothes and trainers, completely unbothered by the fact he had verbally assaulted and threatened Paul and Rich days ago.

The barber shook off the apron, sending hair across the floor. A television is mounted in the corner of the shop for all to view - its volume is excessively high to compensate for the multiple clippers' hum.

A film was playing that had yet to leave the cinema - the quality of the videotape was poor, recorded from the rear of a picture house using a handheld camera.

Posters and flyers advertising raves, food shops and boxing matches are stuck to the walls surrounding each barber's mirrors.

Leon's barber summoned the next customer, and the haircut cycle began again.

Cain pulled up outside in his gun-metal-grey 'Golf GTI', got out and walked into the barbershop.

He walked past three barbers trimming hair and greeted them all before reaching Leon.

Cain lowered himself into a chair next to him.

"What's happening?" Leon asked Cain.

Cain stared at Leon, his expression anything but content, and for a moment, Paul imagined Cain pulling something from his waistband and committing a horrific act upon his foot soldier.

Well, at least he'd already had his haircut for his big day in the dirt, Paul mused, the macabre joke almost pulling laughter from him that would have made him appear as unhinged as the thought.

"You think I'm stupid?" Cain questioned Leon in a whisper, loud enough to overcome the sound of the clippers but lower than the volume of the television.

Leon's brow creased.

"What?" Leon responded.

Cain adjusted himself in the seat to get closer to Leon's ear.

"I told you lot to leave the situation, no? "Cain replied.

Leon maintained his silence, his gaze fixed upon a point on the floor, his expression devoid of emotion.

"I told you I'd handle it, right?" Cain continued.

"I don't know what you're on about, bro," Leon responded.

Cain let out a sigh and closed his eyes, looking up at the ceiling in an overt display of stress.

Paul sat there gazing up at the television, giving the impression he was engrossed in the film rather than their discussion.

"You see what you lot did… It's gonna cause major problems now." Cain stated.

"Bro - I honestly don't know what you're on about." Leon protested.

Cain shook his head.

"Keep playing dumb, yeah; you lot are kids in a big man's game. As my youngers, this all falls on me now..." Cain said, patting his own chest.

"I hope you lot are ready for war?" Cain continued, pointing his finger in Leon's face.

The barber shop door swung open, and Cain spun around with a gasp, pushing his hand under the bottom of his T-shirt and gripping his gun handle.

An elderly Black man entered and approached the customer waiting chairs.

The man greeted each barber as he advanced.

Relaxed, Cain withdrew his hand from beneath his top.

"Pearl's boy, is that you?" The older man asked Cain.

Cain smiled.

"Yes, Herbert," Cain replied.

"How long has it been? Two - three years?" Herbert responded.

"Yeah-I-ah…was away, you know," Cain replied.

"Yes, your mother did tell me, hope you're keeping yourself out of trouble now," Herbert stated, pointing at Cain.

Cain smiled.

"Yeah, I'm at college getting my forklift licence." Cain lied.

Herbert smiled.

"Well, mek sure you keep to it," Herbert responded.

"Will do - Listen, Herbert, it's been nice seeing you, but I've got to shoot, I mean go," Cain said, standing up; Leon mirrored him.

Cain shook Herbert's hand and walked towards the barber's shop entrance, Leon following.

Herbert sat down with a grunt and pulled out a pair of spectacles. He placed them on the tip of his nose, then he retrieved from his pocket a sheet of race-betting newspaper and a pen to select his greyhounds and racehorses.

Paul watched Cain and Leon outside, their heads rotating in all directions as they entered Cain's car.

Herbert exhaled and turned towards Paul; his eyes were dark brown, encircled by milky white rings around the irises. He licked his lips and then used the pen to point at Paul across the two vacated seats.

"You live round here?…" Herbert asked.

Paul wished his barber would hurry up and rescue him from the lecture he was certain he was about to receive.

"I used to. This place was a lot different then - things have changed…Black people don't know how to live good again," Herbert said, then licked his lips like a snake sipping air.

Herbert scanned Paul's face, then swung one leg over the other, and leant in closer.

"You see those boys," Herbert said, pointing at the two chairs vacated by Leon and Cain.

"No good. You, on the other hand, look like you've yet to be spoilt, so let me tell you this: never settle, never feel sorry for yourself - life is the adventure - bigger than where you begin, greater than where you're going. Be bold; find where the river runs to, young man. Oh, and go with good company," Herbert said and nodded as if in agreement with himself.

Paul's frown became a small smile.

"There it is," Herbert said, smiling back; his eyes, although dim, looked like they had once housed an inferno.

"There you are; you're too young to look so old," Herbert continued.

A barber summoned Paul. Paul stood slowly. Him and Herbert maintained eye contact.

"Always remember. You have it; it nah have you, you hear me?" Herbert said in a Jamaican accent.

"Thanks," Paul responded.

The barber summoned Paul again, and Herbert pointed towards the barber, instructing Paul to go. Paul sat in the barber's chair, while Herbert returned to marking his bets.

As Paul's haircut commenced, he closed his eyes and contemplated Herbert's words, and for a fleeting moment, he and Rich were journeying aboard the freight train, in search of its final destination.

Tomorrow

"You hear about the…" Xavier said, making a single gun out of both his hands-shooting at Paul and Fabian.

"Stop that man," Paul said.

"Yeah, can't you see them dutty pigs all over the area?" Fabian responded, looking around.

"You lot know who did, right?" Fabian continued.

Paul started to laugh and shook his head.

"What?" Fabian asked.

Paul laughed even louder.

"What's so funny?" Xavier asked Paul.

"Dirty pigs. Fabs acting like he's some big, big gangster," Paul said.

Fabian shrugged.

"You must have forgotten I'm from here, blud…" Fabian said, his eyelids fluttering.

"No, you're from here, but you are not from the streets. How long have you lived in Harrow?" Paul asked.

"You idiot," Fabian replied.

"Whatever. I know if you got robbed right now, you'd be the first to run to the dutty pigs for help." Paul said, making speech marks over the words 'dutty pigs' with his fingers.

"Nah," Fabian said.

"Nah?" Paul questioned.

"Nah!" Fabian repeated, raising his voice.

Xavier exhaled loudly.

"Come on, you man. Who cares?" Xavier said.

"I do. I hear Rich is moving out as well. Bet you wouldn't tell him the same ting." Fabian responded.

Paul shook his head.

"You're a fool." Paul replied.

Fabian began to chuckle.

Xavier kissed his teeth.

"Oh, now it's your precious little Richard; the rules change, ha? You and him are moving like lovers." Fabian said, laughing.

Paul shook his head; angry flesh swelled around his knuckles.

"Guys, forget all that. I have a house party for us to go to this Saturday. You man in?" Xavier questioned.

Paul stood in silence, staring at Fabian. Fabian looked away from Paul and spoke to Xavier.

"A house party at a time like this? It's gonna kick off, bro. North West is boiling with beef right now, Raphs, right down to Chalk Hill." Fabian reasoned.

"Come on, I'm not stupid. It isn't round here. It's in Peckham." Xavier replied.

"Oh Peckham, even better," Fabian said sarcastically with raised eyebrows.

"Nah, mate - not them parts of Peckham. It's in the posh bits. My brother works with a girl whose dad's an ambassador for Peru. Her parents are away, and she's having a party and wants my bro to run the music down there. Not only that. She wants him to bring a couple guys for her friends." Xavier elaborated, raising both eyebrows up and down.

"Wha! Peru you know! Exotic gullies. You on it?" Fabian asked Paul.

Xavier and Fabian looked to Paul, awaiting his response. Paul did not react; instead, he appeared pensive.

"Come on, P," Fabian said.

"My brother's driving as well; you've got to come; this'll be the last party of summer," Xavier added.

Paul licked his lips and kissed his teeth.

"I don't think my mum will have it. Especially with all the shootings." Paul said.

Fabian tapped Paul's arm to get his attention, as if he did not already have it.

"Just say you're staying over mine," Fabian suggested.

"Yeah, but my madre's gonna want to speak to your mum and all that; trust me, it's long," Paul replied.

"Come on, blud. That's minor. I'll get my sister to cover for you." Fabian reasoned.

Xavier and Fabian looked to Paul for his response.

"Hmmm… Today's what? Wednesday right? If I'm gonna make this happen, I need to work on her from now." Paul explained.

"Well, get to it, dishes, hoovering, whatever. You cannot miss this party, bro. It's gonna be zang." Xavier said.

Two police officers walked around the corner and stood at the top of the road, staring down at the trio standing by the orphanage, Josephine's brother and friends normally stood outside of.

The sun had begun to set, and as of two days ago, a curfew had been in place for 9pm on account of Leon and his gang 'C10' going into Stonebridge estate and shooting rivals, sparking a deadly back and forth between all surrounding council estates in North West London.

Fabian glanced at his watch; it read 7.15pm. The boys looked back at the policemen.

"Why don't they move, man? It's only quarter past seven," Fabian said.

Paul smiled.

"If I'm being honest - I'm cool with them being about," Paul said.

Fabian raised his eyebrows.

"Yeah, I am. Round here's been mad peaceful. No one making noise outside my yard till four in the morning, no fighting or cursing. No drug dealing or worrying about my mum coming in with all these addicts running about. For once in my life, I live somewhere kinda normal." Paul elaborated.

"Ha! You'd love Harrow. Jus old White people and silence," Fabian responded.

Xavier took a deep breath and exhaled.

"You lot are boring, man. I'm going home." Xavier said.

"Yeah, me too, you walking up?" Fabian added and asked Paul.

"Nah, I'm gonna chill here for a bit. Rich said he's coming down before curfew. Oh yeah, is Rich invited?" Paul asked Xavier.

"Come on, blud, of course," Xavier answered.

Paul nodded.

"Cool, I'll let him know," Paul said.

Fabian and Xavier left for home.

Paul walked over to the park and waited forty-five minutes for Rich to arrive, but he never showed up.

The warmth from the last days of summer was beginning to abandon the evenings. Goosebumps covered Paul's arms as he returned from the park under a sky of white, amber, and auburn hues.

As he neared the orphanage, he glanced up at the flats opposite and caught Josephine before she could retreat behind her curtains as usual.

He slowed his pace, the pair engaged in a peculiar stare-off that neither wished to partake in or end.

He broke eye contact first, and when he looked back, Josephine had vanished, and her curtains were closed as if she had never been there.

Summer 1992

Dr. Vincent Appiah entered his sun-drenched garden, bound for his shed at the end.

He had three rusting keys in the back pocket of his beige khaki shorts. He was barefoot and buoyant in mood and step.

He grabbed the small padlock on the paint-peeled shed door and attempted the first key, the second, and finally the third, which unlocked it.

He looked to the sky and rolled his eyes. 'Sod's law,' he whispered.

He rummaged around the clutter inside the shed and emerged with two medium-sized bags of coal.

He walked back over to a wooden fold-out table set up by the back door of his house.

A moment of reflection seized him, and in an instant, he was back in Oyarifa in Ghana - eighteen, wearing hand-me-down clothes and looking up at the impossible scale of Aubri's mountains in the distance, his adolescent mind unable to fathom how he'd ever be able to escape the impoverished paradise that was Ghana, for the promised pavements of gold in the West.

He returned from the flashback to the present, and under the intensity of his vision, he had punctured the bags of coal in several places.

His fingers were black with coal dust. He was annoyed that he had to wash his hands before he dirtied the white tablecloth and his clothes.

Dr. Appiah and his wife, Levette, expected guests to arrive at 1pm. At 12.30, Levette, their son Nana, and their daughter Josephine rushed about in a panic, setting out chairs and decorating two table tops with a medley of juice, water, whisky, wine, malt, bowls of crisps, sweets, and cooked finger food from Jamaica and Ghana.

By 3.30pm, everyone who had been invited was there: Aunt Lucille, her two daughters and son, Dr. Jerry and Ross, to name a few.

The aroma of newly cut grass wrestled with the burning scent of barbecue coals.

Guests had gathered in small groups, and the sound of carefree human chatter carried across the garden in Hanwell.

Josephine, aged ten, plays with her cousins, family and friends

As Josephine rushed past her father, who was tending the grill and conversing with colleagues, he gently grabbed his daughter's shoulder and said, "Yɛ ahwɛyie, darling".

Josephine smiled and continued at a brisk pace to appease him.

Josephine and her friends dug in the sun-baked mud with plastic knives and forks taken from the tables, searching for worms they would never find.

Suddenly, Josephine heard a loud gasp behind her, which drew her attention.

She observed her father trembling uncontrollably, gripping the scorching sides of the barbecue as if he were a contestant on some morbid, death-defying game show where competitors had to see who could endure holding the heated grill the longest.

Vincent suddenly stopped shaking and became as rigid as board, fell forwards then backwards, dragging the grill down upon himself.

The party guests gasped and crowded around him in a huddle.

Josephine stood up and hurried towards them. She pushed through and peered down at her father, whose mouth was drooping on one side. He was holding the hot grill mesh to his chest.

Coal, chicken and ash covered him, raising burning sores across his bare thighs and searing through his cotton T-shirt.

His hands were swollen and severely burnt.

Josephine's mother is kneeling by her husband, frantically sweeping glowing coals off his body, her eyes trembling, red and watering.

Levette is telling her husband in frantic shrieks that all will be alright. Dr. Jerry used a paper towel in each hand to remove the grill mesh from Vincent's grip.

Dr. Ross sprinted towards the house to call an ambulance.

The remaining guests fell into an unsettling silence.

Vincent is making gurgling sounds that Josephine shall never forget. He is in agony, and she begins to weep.

Her elder brother Nana has his hands on top of his head, sobbing, being escorted away and consoled by Aunt Lucille, who is doing her best to shield his vision from the dreadful sight that has become her brother-in-law.

Dr. Vincent Appiah would die of a stroke on his birthday - 12th August 1992.

The man who had overcome so much to make it to the UK had been wiped out by a concoction of stress and unhealthy foods.

That day changed everything for Nana, Josephine, and Levette. Their rock and talisman was gone, leaving them with no one to orbit, plunging their privileged lives into a violent free fall.

The king of wishful thinking

"I had to move my shift to nine because of the curfew, so I'll be back at seven. Start getting your brother ready for bed at around half-past six, okay."

"Will do. Anything else?" Paul said.

Paul's mum stood by the front door looking at her son, one arm in her cardigan, the other free.

"Errr… What's going on?" Paul's mother asked.

Paul shrugged.

"What do you mean?" Paul responded.

Paul's mum squinted, pursing her lips.

"Will do…" She repeated.

Even Paul could not help but smile at how it must have appeared to her, given that no less than two days prior, he had made a tremendous fuss about having to look after his brother all the time.

She slid her other arm into the cardigan and began fixing her attire.

"What are you looking for? If it's money, I don't have it," she said.

Paul shifted his posture.

"He wants to go to a party with his friends!" Paul's younger brother Jermaine screamed from above.

Paul and his mum looked up the staircase, then at each other.

"Party! At a time like this! With all these shootings, no way," his mum said, shaking her head.

"Na-na, no, it's not a party. It's a sleepover at Fabian's house," Paul said, cutting in, fighting for clarity, knowing that if she said 'no,' his mother was a very hard woman to reverse.

Her face became thoughtful.

"Fabian… Isn't that Norma's from up the tops son?" She asked.

"Yeah, but they moved to Harrow, remember. There's no problems down there," Paul clarified.

She began to squint; *this is good*, he thought. It meant she was fifty-fifty.

"Get Norma to call me," she requested.

"I can't, his mum's away -"

"A-way!" Paul's mum repeated, her eyes as wide as the sky.

Paul went into a state of panic. That irreversible 'no' was coming down the pipe fast and had to be stopped.

"Yeah, but his sister will be in charge - she's twenty-five." Paul reasoned.

"Twenty-five!" His mum said.

Oh, come on, twenty-five doesn't deserve repeating, Paul thought.

His mother fell silent, staring through her son.

"Hmm. I'll let you know after I speak with his sister."

"Okay," Paul said.

His mother took a deep breath and opened the front door.

"Make sure you look after your brother properly, or you aren't going anywhere. And I don't want you two sitting on that Nintendo all day. Get some fresh air. You hear me?"

"Yes mum," Paul replied.

"No back chat from you today, ha?" His mum responded, cackling as she went through the front door, her perfume trailing her like runaway bunting would wind.

When Paul turned around, his brother Jermaine was standing five steps up from the floor, gazing down upon him.

Paul shook his head from side to side in disgust at the manner in which his brother had divulged his plans.

"Remember what Mum said...." Jermaine reasoned, wanting to prevent any reprisals Paul may have had in store.

*****

At 10.30am, the sun was blazing; it must have been at least 30 degrees outside, and Zion had come up to Paul's balcony and was asking him to go out.

"You wanna go check Slim?" Zion asked.

"Nah. I can't. I'm looking after my brother today," Paul said, turning around to look into the living room where Jermaine was sitting, legs crossed, his face right up to the TV screen, game controller in hand, moving a little red Italian man jumping up and down across land, water and green pipes.

"Bring him," Zion suggested.

"Ta Slims!? You must be mad!" Paul replied.

Zion sighed.

"This summer's been whack, man. This curfew ting, and no one wants to do anything," Zion moaned, before leaving.

At 11.10am - Alicia knocked for Paul. Paul answered the door.

"What you up to?" Alicia asked.

"I'm making lunch," Paul replied, annoyed.

His brother was making a considerable racket in the background, leaping about with two toys in hand—Leonardo, the leader of the teenage mutant hero turtles, doing battle with his nemesis, Shredder.

Alicia tried peering beyond Paul inside. Paul moved into her line of sight with each attempt.

"Your mum in?" Alicia asked.

"No. Why?" Paul replied.

"Do you want me to help you look after your brother? I'm a good cook," Alicia asked and stated, dreamy-eyed.

"Nah, I got it," Paul responded.

She looked Paul up and down, his bare chest on display.

"So, are you still with Maria, then?" Alicia asked, beaming—she was already in receipt of the answer.

Paul rolled his eyes and exhaled a sigh.

"No. Look, I need to get back to making lunch," Paul said, pointing behind himself.

"Alright, chill," Alicia responded, adjusting her skirt.

Paul gazed past her.

"Why won't you give us a chance, though?" Alicia pleaded.

"Us! Oh, here we go again," Paul moaned.

By 1pm, Jermaine was all played out, had eaten, and was napping on the sofa. Xavier and Paul sat in Paul's kitchen, eating Space Raiders and penny sweets from the Rothmans corner shop.

"So, you coming on Saturday?" Xavier asked.

Paul lowered and raised his hand through the air, gesturing for Xavier to keep his voice down.

Paul peered around the kitchen door into the living room at his brother, who was still fast asleep.

"I spoke to my mum this morning, and it's looking kinda good. She wanted to speak to Fabian's mum; I told her she's away, but his sister's about." Paul said.

Xavier rubbed his hands together in glee.

"Don't celebrate too soon. I gotta keep him happy, or it ain't happening," Paul said, thumbing towards the living room.

"Easy peasy," Xavier replied.

Xavier pulled out a pack of red 'Maryland' cookies. Paul laughed.

"What?.. Kids can't resist 'em," Xavier stated.

"Oh yeah?" Paul replied, snatching the cookies off him.

The letterbox clanged once more, disrupting the silence; Paul nearly leapt to the ceiling to get to the door before it woke his brother.

"What!!!" Paul hissed as he pulled open the front door.

Needless to say, Pastor Tion was thoroughly unamused at being greeted in this manner. Consequently, Xavier, Paul and Jermaine were made to sit in the living room and endure an hour of scripture and lecture on the importance of having manners and 'blasted respect".

Xavier departed shortly after the pastor.

Paul regarded Jermaine, who shook his head in disapproval. In response, Paul produced the packet of cookies, and Jermaine began to smile.

They shared the cookies and watched 'Back To The Future' again, the beginning and end, as the middle of the videotape had been corrupted.

Jermaine went to the toilet and returned.

"I'm bored," Jermaine announced.

"Bored?" Paul repeated.

"Uh-huh," Jermaine replied.

"Okay. You want to go to the park for a bit?" Paul offered.

"Yeah."

They left at 4pm. Outside was lovely.

A cool breeze accompanied them. They passed two police officers on patrol, and further along the road near the park, a police van was parked. All doors were open, and five officers were inside, shirts unbuttoned, frantically fanning themselves.

At the park, Jermaine hurried to grab one of the many abandoned milk crates to use on the long metal slide.

Paul watched his brother and two other young boys lugging the brown crates up the slope.

One child slid down the slide, then the next, without waiting for the previous person to disembark. Paul shook his head with a 'tut' and turned towards the swings, and there she was, staring in his direction.

As soon as she realised, he had realised—she looked away. Initially, he was going to stay put, but something compelled him towards her like a moth to moonlight.

Josephine's brother (Nana, also known as Jungle) was a 'C10' gang member, and talking to her would be seen by most as asking for serious trouble, an interaction best avoided.

Paul walked up and sat one swing away from Josephine.

She looked away from him in the direction of her flat.

Jermaine and his newfound friends were now playing 'had' and creating quite a racket.

Paul summoned courage.

"Josephine, right?" Paul asked.

Josephine stopped rocking in the swing and turned towards him. When he saw her face - which was dark brown and beautiful - he immediately felt a flutter in his stomach.

"Yeah. And you're Paul."

Paul frowned.

"How'd you know my name?" He asked, swaying in his swing.

"Same way you know mine." She responded.

The pair fell silent, staring at each other before displaying matching smiles.

"Sorry," she continued.

"For what?" Paul responded.

"For being sarcastic."

Paul frowned.

"Sar-what?" he asked.

"Don't worry about it," she said.

Paul stared at her mouth and lips.

"Why are you looking at me like that?" Josephine said in response to his unflinching gaze.

"Nah, it's jus…Just you talk like you're not from round here. How come?"

She looked above Paul's brow in thought.

"You really want to know?"

"Yeah," Paul replied.

"On one condition," Josephine said.

"Okay."

"Don't ask me about my brother or the…You know."

Paul nodded to reassure her.

"I wouldn't have anyway. " Paul responded.

Besides, Paul thought, everyone *knows C10 are on the run for the SBG shootings, and Jungle, AKA Nana, your brother, flew to Ghana to escape.*

Josephine recounted to Paul how her life transitioned from privilege to poverty following her father's passing, resulting in her mother suffering from dreadful mental health issues, leading to them losing their home and income, culminating in them becoming council tenants.

Paul stared at the floor, thinking about what he had just been told.

"That's mad..." Paul murmured.

"Sorry - I don't even know you, and I'm telling you all my problems," Josephine said.

"It's cool, I asked."

They fell silent together, Paul's mind processing her almost unimaginable tale of tragedy. Josephine glanced at her watch, then at Paul.

"I need to go. My mum gets home soon, and I haven't started dinner," Josephine said.

She rose and adjusted her clothes.

"I'll see you around, ha?" Josephine stated.

"Yeah, I guess so," Paul replied.

"Bye." Josephine said as she turned to walk home.

Paul glanced back at his brother, who was back on the slide. Paul's mind was filled with a medley of thoughts and things to say to her before she was out of earshot, and before he could think it through, it flew out of his mouth.

"Josephine!" Paul shouted.

Josephine stopped and turned to face him.

"You, err...You want to come to a party this Saturday?"

Josephine looked befuddled.

"I mean, I know you don't know me, but.. But I err, I err, think you could do with it." Paul reasoned with a shrug of his shoulders.

"Party? Where?" Josephine said.

"South London. Got a lift as well," Paul assured.

Josephine examined his face. He looked at her the way her father used to look at her.

"What time does it start and finish?" Josephine asked.

Paul smiled unexpectedly, pleased that she was considering the proposition.

"Starts at seven, probably finishes two, maybe threeish," Paul replied.

Josephine had lived on the estate for three years and sparingly conversed with a few girls who also lived there, and that was solely because they attended her secondary school.

The people in her area were far from her kind of people. "Typical of the environment," she would often say to her two privately educated cousins from Cambridge, who were fascinated by Josephine's new life and often called to get updates on her *drug dealer and addict* diary entries.

Her brother's gang affiliation meant boys would not even dare look in her direction, let alone talk to her - this was one positive outcome of her brother's troubled adolescence, she often reasoned, trying to find a glimmer of light in his darkness.

When Nana began down his path of self-destruction, her mother clung to her, which resulted in Josphine's every movement being managed and monitored.

Her mother feared Josephine might go astray and become entangled in her brother's trajectory.

Consequently, Josephine was unable to socialise like other fifteen-year-olds - the only party she could recollect attending was the one her father never made it out of.

Although her brother and mother were locked in a troubled relationship owing to Nana's life choices, they were united in suppressing her social life.

With her brother now on the run - and her mother surprisingly upbeat in his absence, it felt like her cell door had been left open, tempting her to do something reckless and make a run for it.

"I'll let you know tomorrow," Josephine said.

"Right, I mean...Okay. Should we meet here at the same time? " Paul asked.

"Yeah, that can work." She replied, walking backwards before turning towards her home, her smile bigger than his.

Paul watched her walk up to her house. She took one last look over, then opened her front door and went in. At that moment, Paul realised two things: he was holding his breath and was officially playing with fire.

Paul's father, Jacob Hawk

On 12th November 1955, Jacob Hawk was fourteen years old and had endured a challenging twenty-two days at sea.

Jacob's appointed caretaker on board, Nelson Cannon, developed cabin fever and attempted to jump into the Atlantic with Jacob in his arms due to his condition.

Needless to say, for his own and everyone else's safety, Nelson had to be confined for the remainder of the journey to England, leaving Jacob reliant on staff (who, frankly, were not particularly welcoming towards people of colour), and fellow passengers—elders and neighbours from his Parish in St Elizabeth.

Like many from the Caribbean, Jacob's mother Paulette and his father Cuthbert had answered the 'Motherland's' call and departed Jamaica for England five years prior.

Paulette worked as a nurse, and Cuthbert worked on the buses. After several years of renting a house with two and, at times, three other families, they finally saved up enough money and found an agent willing to sell homes to Blacks.

They purchased and renovated a dilapidated three-bedroom house in Willesden.

Once the house was in satisfactory condition, they sent for Jacob and asked Paulette's cousin, Marcia, who was staying with them, to collect him and Nelson from Tilbury docks - situated in Essex.

Marcia was eighteen, well-dressed, tall and incredibly thin. Her complexion was remarkably darker than Jacob's.

She looked fed up and exhausted, pulling one of Jacob's suitcases along the rough cobbled street. Jacob, following behind, fumbling with three cloth bags.

Jacob surveyed his surroundings, absorbing the motherland. He wondered if the ship had docked in the wrong country, as it was freezing and everything looked so grey—a far cry from the green and pleasant land he and many had envisaged.

Marcia glanced over her shoulder at her young cousin and spoke through large plumes of breath vapour.

"Don't talk ta heenyone, and don't mek eye contact with White people." She said in her thick Jamaican accent.

"Why?" Jacob asked.

"Them nah like we."

"Bah-" Jacob began.

"Nah budda hask heenymore question. Just do has-I-say. "

The concept of England was quickly surpassing the reality for Jacob.

"You are light-skinned but no longer privileged—England is a great leveller, lickle bwoy," Marcia said. Her eyes glistened, and her mouth formed what appeared to be a crescent of joy or something far more sinister. She frightened him.

He yearned to get back on the boat and return home, like Nelson, his maddened carer, was being forced to do - he was not the only one who desired this either.

Jacob and Marcia stood with a large group of Caribbeans at a coach stand. Across the road from the bus stop, a group of over twenty white men were waving placards, with a few police officers keeping them in place.

At first, Jacob thought it was a welcome committee until he read some of the vile things written on their signs. *Monkeys go home. England for the English. No Blacks. No dogs. No Irish.*

Jacob caught the eye of one of the men, and the man shouted something Jacob couldn't understand. Marcia struck Jacob on the head.

"What did I say?" Marcia hissed.

An elder man, a fellow passenger from the ship, seized Marcia's hand, which was about to strike Jacob once more.

"Oi! Don't hangle him like that. Uh-nah fi him fault." The man said.

Marcia dropped the scowl and became prim and proper.

"Oh, but sir, we-nah-wan-nah problem," she responded.

The man released a long sigh. *He's been in the country for an hour, and he was already sighing like that, not a good sign* - Jacob thought.

"He's not the problem! These people are," the man said, his statement eliciting murmurs from the rest.

Suddenly, two bricks came flying from the agitators, and chaos erupted.

Punches, sticks, suitcases, and kicks were flying everywhere.

Outnumbered, the police could do little else but stand back and let the disturbance run its course.

What a start to life in England. What a start for Paul's father-to-be.

Small lie, big adventure

Biggie Smalls's rap song, 'One More Chance,' plays, and Fabian is standing in the centre of the room, rapping along with the lyrics and swaying to the beat.

Paul screwed up his face and then kissed his teeth. "Shut up, Fabian," Paul said, rolling tobacco, sat on the edge of Slim's bed.

Xavier and Rich collapsed in laughter. Fabian looked down at Paul, unamused.

"You're a hater," Fabian said.

"Blud - you're always rapping over Biggie; we don't wanna hear that. We wanna hear Big." Paul protested.

"Oh-ya! You will this Saturday... Xavier's brother wants me ta emcee at the party. Uh-lie X?" Fabian asked Xavier.

All eyes turned to Xavier for confirmation. Xavier nodded.

"Wait? What! But you're rubbish!" Slim said, spinning around from his two turntables, headphones hanging off one ear.

"Forget you lot. I know I'm good," Fabian protested.

"Yeah, but can you spit over House and G, bro? Like, you know, original lyrics and that?" Rich asked.

Fabian watched Paul drink from a water bottle, raise his eyebrows, and smirk.

"Your uh fool, you know that?" Fabian said, shaking his head at Paul.

"Why are you talking to me? I didn't say a word." Paul responded.

"Okay, watch. Slim, hook up the mic." Fabian demanded.

Slim smiled. "Alright then," Slim responded.

Slim handed Fabian the mic and put on a track (Q-Rius—Spread Love). The beat got everyone bubbling! Fabian began nodding his head to the beat and, after a few seconds, pulled a face.

"Nah, this ain't it," Fabian said over the mic.

Slim looked over at Fabian.

"Too soft. Give me something harder than that," Fabian asked.

Slim nodded, spun the vinyl back, and placed another record on the opposite turntable.

The track is (New Horizons - Put Your Mouth On Me). Fabian began to rock his head. Paul lit the roll-up, took a deep drag, and then released a cloud of smoke into the room. Rich and Xavier's heads were bopping to the beat.

"Okay! Okay! The name is F, A ta the B. I stands for incredible emcee! And A… Stands for Amazing. And N means Paul can never test me. Harles-dun, is where I come from, where all the men dem get gyal for fun, son!" Fabian rapped - pointing at Paul.

Paul shook his head.

Xavier and Rich erupted into a uniform "OOOOOOOOO!" jumping on top of each other and rocking Slim's bed from side to side.

Paul looked on at Fabian, smiling at him.

Fabian offered Paul the microphone.

Being lyrically challenged, Paul grinned and ignored the offer, knowing he had no comeback to the lyric.

Fabian brought the microphone to his mouth and spoke to Paul through it.

"I told you, fool! Just pass me the roll-up!" Fabian's said. His voice boomed out of the speakers. The entire neighbourhood must have heard him. Slim spun around, lowering the volume of the music and the microphone, the fear of God etched into his face.

"Fab! You can't be saying th-." Before Slim could finish his sentence, the staircase outside his room came to life, drawing everyone's attention to Slim's closed bedroom door.

Paul tossed the roll-up over his shoulder out of the window into Slim's garden below, and everyone sprang up - flapping their hands, attempting to push the smoke towards the open windows.

Slim's elder sister Fay pushed Slim's bedroom door open - wincing at the smell.

"Andre, a word, now!" She said, scanning the room.

Slim removed the headphones from over his head and left. Everyone kept their heads lowered. Rich glanced up first and started giggling into his palms, which got everyone else going.

Paul looked over at Fabian and shook his head - Fabian pulled a face. After the muffled sound of reprimanding, Slim returned to the room, his face upset, and everyone had to leave.

They exited his house in single file; Fay stood by the front door in her black, blue and purple NatWest bank uniform - neck tie and all, as if she were their concierge.

The boys came out to Ade and Giant sat on Slim's wall, wondering why they could not go in.

Last out, Rich turned to Fay and said, "Sorry, Fay." Fay turned away from him, grumbling and slammed the front door in his face.

They all stood in silence.

"Wow! Fay looks peeved. What happened?" Ade asked.

"Ask him," Xavier said, pointing at Fabian.

Giant began to laugh, and Paul followed suit.

"Put it this way, me and Slim ain't going to that party tomorrow," Rich added.

"Swear," Ade replied.

Fabian tutted.

"He said his sister wouldn't be back until five—didn't he, P?" Fabian protested, looking to Paul to garner support for his argument.

"Five…Five…" Paul said to himself as he squinted.

"Innit, that's what he said." Fabian continued, looking at each of his friends.

Then it dawned on him - and Paul remembered his meeting with Josephine.

"I need to go," Paul exclaimed.

"Where?" Rich asked.

"I need to meet someone."

"Is it? What's her name, then? She got friends?" Ade asked.

Paul smiled.

"Wha! You got a gully?" Rich added.

"Nah, not even?" Paul responded, smiling from ear to ear.

"Bare grinning, you know. If it ain't a gyal, it's got ta be money." Ade said.

Paul laughed. "Listen, I gotta go. X, you sure I can bring someone in Rich's place?" Paul asked Xavier, stepping backwards.

"As long as they're cool, it's cool," Xavier responded.

"You're defo taking a girl tomorrow," Rich said.

Paul shrugged in response.

Fabian grinned. "Just make sure she ain't ugly like the ones you normally get." Fabian insisted.

Paul gave him the middle finger, turned, and went to meet Josephine.

✱✱✱✱✱

As the summer drew to a close and following several prominent gang-related arrests, the police presence in the area began to diminish. As a result, and unseen for weeks, undesirable elements had begun to resurface.

Josephine sat up in her vantage point overlooking the park, where Paul had promised to meet her thirty minutes ago.

Instead, she observed one of her subjects, Head-back Hattie—a slight, White woman—walking in and out of the swings and up the slide's cement slope, where she stood at its summit, looking at the train tracks the way Paul would with his friends.

The curfew had created a problem for drug dealers and takers - supply and demand, unable to meet in peace. Josephine sat with a new page for Hattie in her drug takers' journal. But nothing came.

She couldn't get her mind off Paul and the fact that she was convinced he had played her like a fiddle - *Probably laughing with his friends right now*, she thought. Laughing at the fact that she would dare think she could transcend her status as a fatherless drug dealer's sister. She began to regret trusting him with her story.

She groaned, crossed her arms over her desk and diary, and rested her head.

Before she could close her eyes, an object struck her window.

She raised her head and looked out.

Paul was stood below, a few pebbles in hand; he appeared as though he had run a marathon - his chest rising and falling rapidly. He gestured for her to open the window.

She didn't. She watched him. He gestured once more - In response, she tapped an imaginary watch on her wrist.

He appeared dejected. He brought his hands together as if praying, and mouthed, 'Sorry.'

She wished to be upset with him, but his persistence drew her lips apart, forming a small smile. She signalled that she was coming down.

She stood up and walked towards her bedroom door, a spring in her step.

She slowed as she reached her wardrobe mirror, where she ran her hands through her hair. She reached for a pot of lotion from her bed and ensured her face was creamed and presentable. *Hold on; he's just a friend, right?* Josephine pondered, massaging her face with cocoa butter.

She looked at her sweet-smelling brown skin in the mirror - *Can't be anything more, can he? Of course not.* she responded to herself. *Then what's that humming here?* She glanced down at her stomach, shut her eyes to quell the thoughts, and proceeded to the door.

She made sure to tread the stairs gently, as her mother worked night shifts and was not pleasant when tired.

She opened her front door and discovered that Paul had been cornered by Hattie.

"Move, man, I ain't got no drugs," Paul stated.

"Come on, babe. You must know someone? I got the money." Hattie replied, pulling a fistful of five and ten-pound notes out of her jeans pocket.

Paul looked down at her palm - the notes were crumpled and sullied. He shook his head and shrugged.

"I can't help you..." Paul insisted.

Hattie groaned and then looked past Paul towards Josephine.

"Your brother about?" Hattie asked.

Josephine appeared mortified.

"You better leave before I call the police," Josephine responded, pointing at a police van parked up the road in the distance.

Hattie stepped back, raised her hands in surrender, turned and walked away. The pair watched her leave. Paul tutted.

"Don't you recognise her?" Josephine asked.

Paul looked puzzled.

"No? Look. She normally looks like this when she's had a hit."

Josephine swung her head back, opened her mouth and eyes wide, and walked around in a circle, gazing upwards. Paul raised his hand to his mouth to suppress his laughter.

"No way. Is that her?!" Paul questioned.

"Yep," Josephine replied.

Paul looked back at where Hattie had gone, his smile slowly vanishing, his brow wrinkled with waves of thought.

"You okay?" Josephine asked.

Paul looked back at Josephine.

"Man, I hate this place at times," Paul whispered as if he didn't want to say it.

Josephine remained motionless for several seconds.

"At times? Is that all?" She responded.

A large cloud moved across the sky and obscured the sun, diminishing its light.

"You want to go over," Paul said, nodding towards the park.

They strolled to the swings and sat side by side.

A group of girls emerged from the cemetery entrance, which linked the park to St Mary's Church, after which the road and housing estate were named.

The group walked by them, hair gelled down in finger waves across their foreheads and down their sideburns, like 'Lil Kim' and 'Missy Elliot'.

Their eyebrows were raised as they whispered and giggled at Paul and Josephine's meeting.

"Hey, P." Ronda, one of the group's girls, said as they moved past.

"Whagwan?" Paul replied.

Ronda slowed and began to walk backwards to face him.

"Nothing; you lot coming up top to the festival in Acorn tomorrow?" Ronda asked of Paul and the rest of his friends.

"Nah," Paul replied.

"Busy, yeah?" Ronda responded, pointing between him and Josephine.

"Bye, Ronda," Paul replied, trying to contain his smile, his face suddenly felt warm.

"Ba-" Ronda began.

"Byeee!" Paul said, cutting her response.

Ronda winked, turned around and went on her way.

Josephine frowned.

"You seem really popular with the ladies," Josephine stated.

Paul was well-mannered, well-built, handsome, and generally studious. Girls simply adored him.

"Nah, not me." He lied, blushing.

Josephine raised both eyebrows.

"So," Josephine said.

"So?" Paul repeated.

"Aren't you worried?" Josephine replied.

"About?" Paul responded.

"People seeing you with me?"

Paul paused in thought.

"Should I be?" Paul questioned. His heart began to beat rapidly. Scared of her response, afraid of her saying something that would discontinue what appeared to be the beginnings of something.

"No, you shouldn't. My brother isn't here. He's gone to Ghana; we don't know where," she said, watching her trainers stroke the gravel beneath her swing.

Paul didn't react. She looked at Paul's profile.

"I mean. You know. Like… There's no need to worry about anything happening to you. If you are worried about that," Josephine assured.

Paul smiled.

"I'm not." Paul replied, relaxed.

Josephine nodded to this.

"Where's your brother today?" She asked, wanting to move the conversation on.

"His dad's," Paul responded.

"Oh, you have different fathers?"

"Yeah," Paul replied.

"Okay. What about your dad?" Josephine questioned.

Paul shook his head.

"Don't see him much," Paul said.

"Sorry," Josephine replied.

"For what?" Paul said, acting as if it didn't bother him.

"Bringing it up," she responded with a shrug.

"Trust me, I'm good. Anyway, are you coming tomorrow or not?" Paul asked - his turn to change the course of the conversation.

"As long as we can leave here after six, I'm in."

"Why after six?"

"My mum leaves for work at six and doesn't return till five in the morning," Josephine explained.

"So you're gonna lie?" Paul said.

Josephine laughed.

"Errr yeah! Does your mum know you're going?" Josephine responded.

"Nah, I'm at Fabian's, you get me," Paul said with a cheeky wink.

Josephine shook her head.

"Anyway, the Party finishes at two; I'll get you back before your mum gets in," Paul assured.

"Cool," Josephine said.

Paul looked at her wristwatch.

"I gotta go. Where should I meet you tomorrow?" Paul asked, trying to keep his cool as if he wasn't jumping about with joy inside.

"Where's the car picking you up from?" Josephine asked.

"Round the back of the shops - across the road. You want us to come get you?"

"No way. My neighbours can't see me get in a car full of boys. I'll meet you over there - what time?"

"Six forty-five," Paul said.

"Six forty-five it is."

"Wicked," Paul replied, standing up from the swing.

Josephine also stood.

"Thanks," Josephine said.

"No need to thank me."

They both fell silent.

"Friends," Josephine announced, holding her hand out for him to shake.

Paul smiled.

"Friends," Paul repeated and shook her hand, holding on a little longer than he should have - she didn't complain.

✳✳✳✳✳

Later that night, Paul lay in his bed, observing a tiny insect traversing the network of cracks across the plaster of his ceiling.

The bug could have chosen any one of the routes, yet it selected the path leading towards the dimmed light.

With Rich leaving, Josephine felt like that to Paul, like light luring him, pulling him through a system of dark tunnels he had been trying to find the end of since birth.

Paul did not deem Josephine any more or less attractive than the likes of Ronda or Alicia, yet Josephine was different. He loved the fact that she possessed a past connection to a better place outside of there. This instilled him with hope.

Paul turned onto his side, closed his eyes, and started to fall asleep, murmuring, "Be bold... Fi.. Fi.. Find where the river runs, ta, ga. Ga. go with… good comp -" Before he could finish Herbert's words - sleep took him under its spell.

Josephine lay in bed, listening to the freight train rumbling past, leaving serene silence in its wake.

She contemplated her brother and pondered whether he could have shot someone or was merely present.

She reflected upon her mother trying her best to keep their lives together - being both right and wrong in limiting her adolescent endeavours.

She considered her father and how distressed he would be with their living and social circumstances.

She thought about her father's final words to her: "Yɛ ahwɛyie, darling". This shattered her resolve; and alone in the darkness, she wept until slumber overcame her.

As Josephine and Paul slept in anticipation of the party, the universe would unveil a grander adventure for them.

Tomorrow, two canaries shall escape the coal mine, venturing out into the wider world and in one night, embark on a voyage of self-discovery, fantasy, danger and disbelief through and across Central and West London. Encountering peculiar people and creatures that shall endeavour to assist and impede them.

As they slept, the universe would align their paths and bind the pair to a tale they would never believe was true if they hadn't experienced it.

Saturday

Although it was the end of Summer, it was as if it had restarted—bright cloudless, blue skies stretched for as far as the eye could see—and it was warm. Bees and insects flew in and about themselves outside.

Josephine's mother hummed along to a reggae song on the radio as she prepared her dinner for work.

Josephine tiptoed to and stood by the kitchen door, observing her mother, who had her back to her.

Her mother suddenly froze and stared out into their garden.

"It's rude to enter a room unannounced, young lady," Levette said, turning to face her daughter.

"Oh my goodness! I was so quiet. How do you do that?" Josephine questioned with a smile.

"I'm uh, Jamaican," Levette announced.

Josephine rolled her eyes.

"I have news," Levette said, waving the large kitchen knife she used to cut carrots for her salad.

"News?" Josephine said, walking into the kitchen and sitting at the small dining table in the middle of the room - praying her mother wouldn't yell "Surprise, I'm not going to work today!"

"I had a call from the police - your brother has been caught and will be returned."

Josephine stared at her mother, speechless.

*****

Levette stood by the front door, her hand clasped on the door latch, about to leave for her shift. She froze, then turned around as if someone had called her name - Josephine was standing at the kitchen entrance. Her mother appeared to stare through her; her mother's mouth moved as if it did not belong to her.

"Herbert is coming to...drop some...thing. Off for me at... siii..six thirty. Make sure you're... in." Levette said in a slur.

Josephine stepped forward, her face fashioned with concern.

"Mum..." Josephine announced.

Levette shook her head, her eyelids fluttering. She brought her hand to her breastbone and massaged between it and her voice box.

"Oh my, what was that?" Levette questioned.

Josephine rushed towards her mother and embraced her.

"Mum...you okay?"

Levette smiled.

"I'm fine, I'm fine. Just had a weird brain fog. Herbert's coming over at 6.30, so make sure you're in, and the radio is low enough to hear the door. "

A veil of guilt washed over Josephine as she gazed into her mother's eyes, knowing she would disobey her that night.

"Yes, I, I, I mean, of course," Josephine said in a stutter.

Her mother regarded her with suspicion.

"You sure?" Levette questioned, probing.

"Sure," Josephine said, more relaxed, trying to appear as normal as possible.

"Okay," Levette said and walked out. Josephine shut the door behind her mother and leant against it, her head tilted back, her eyes shut. She was unaccustomed to deception, particularly towards her mother.

The stress was almost overwhelming.

*****

"Xavier's brother's gonna drop us there, and Fabian's sister said she'll drop us back early tomorrow. There's no need to stress. " Paul said.

"That's my job. What's the exact time she's getting you back?" Paul's mother asked.

"She said nine or ten in the morning," Paul replied, his hands feeling sweaty.

Paul's mum looked at him from the corner of her eye.

"There's something you're not telling me; I don't know what it is, but there's something." She said, wagging her finger.

*****

A radio sounded in the background. Sunlight flooded Josephine's bedroom.

Josephine held a navy dress and cream cardigan against herself in the mirror.

Once her outfit was selected, she sat on the edge of her bed and tried on two different shoes, comparing them. She went with the white Rebook classics.

With her footwear selected, she began playing around with her hair - dancing and humming to 'Boyz

To Men' in the mirror. She slowed to a stop, but her reflection took a moment longer to catch up.

Josephine froze.

She then bent forward, staring at herself in the mirror for a while.

Then, she looked behind her, and down the corridor towards her mother's room, her mother's door was closed, and the passageway was dim.

Josephine squinted, poked her reflection's eye, and tapped the mirror's glass.

"What the?" she whispered.

*****

"At the third stroke, the time sponsored by Accurist will be - Seventeen forty-five PM...BEEP!"

Paul placed the telephone in its cradle. This was one of ten calls he had made to the speaking clock that day.

A call he would not have had to make had he and his brother not broken their mother's wall clock whilst playing catch with a tennis ball last month; the clock was now permanently stuck at 14:08.

Paul's mother was seated watching 'The New Adventures of Superman' whilst eatting her dinner.

Paul approached the living room door and stood in the doorway.

He was about to speak when he noticed something peculiar. The broken clock on the wall had begun to tick, but its hands were moving backwards and forwards, ticking in opposing directions. He watched it for a few seconds, focused intently, unable to hear his mother speaking.

"Paul!"

"Errr.. yeah," Paul responded, looking down at her.

"What's got into you?" His mother questioned.

Paul looked up at the clock again, pointing at it, but it was once more stuck at 14:08.

He took a sharp breath.

His mother looked at what he was pointing at, then turned her attention back to him.

"Yes, my blasted clock, you lot broke. What about it?"   Paul's mum protested.

Paul's eyes darted around the room.

"Paul!"

"That clock was, was - working," Paul said.

They both looked at the clock and then at each other.

"Son, if you're on drugs, you need to let me know so I can help you." Paul's mum said, sitting forward on the sofa.

"It was, I swear!" Paul protested.

✳ ✳ ✳ ✳ ✳

At 6.30, Josephine's doorbell chimed. She ran downstairs and peered through the peephole. Then, she opened the door.

Herbert was standing there in the warm daylight, wearing his customary broad grin.

"Hey, Jo. You alright?" Herbert asked.

No, she wasn't, she wanted to say. She was on the verge of betraying her mother's trust, and either she was losing her sanity, or her reflection had taken on a life of its own.

She could feel the truth fighting for egress. She wanted to share her bizarre experience with anyone, hoping they would reassure her that it was merely a figment of her imagination.

"I need to drop this off for Mum," Herbert said. He held a small book out for her to take.

The book's cover was made of brown leather, with brown-tinged pages inside. The lettering on the cover was gilded.

She accepted it and examined the title.

'THE WORLD WILL SEE YOU NOW '.

She looked up at Herbert, his smile broader than before, a smile that conveyed - *I know everything, yet nothing at all.*

Josephine's mother had enlisted the services of Herbert when her father passed away. The local Caribbean community claimed that Herbert could transmit and receive messages to and from the afterlife and beyond.

Josephine and her brother were unconvinced, but it appeared to bring their mother happiness, and that was all that mattered.

Herbert looked Josephine up and down.

"Hmmm. You look like you're about to find something that has been lost for a while," Herbert said.

The hair on Joesphine's neck stood erect. She nibbled her lower lip and swallowed.

"Sorry?" She replied.

He did not respond; instead, he shifted his weight from one foot to the other and regarded her through narrowed eyes, as if she were difficult to see.

He raised a finger to his lips and then smiled behind it.

"Take care, Josephine... Both of you," Herbert said, turning on his heels, humming back to his car.

Josephine stood on the doorstep watching him, wanting to dash out and demand he explain what he meant by "both of you." *Me and my brother?* She thought. *My mum?* But deep down, she knew who he was referring to, which somewhat unsettled her.

Shadows under a dipping moon

Fabian, Xavier and Slim stood by Xavier's brother's car, parked on a side street behind Church Road's parade of shops, awaiting Paul and his mysterious guest.

Xavier's brother was polishing and tidying the interior of his white Ford XR2-I.

A tape cassette played jungle music to which they all bobbed their heads.

The sun had begun its descent.

The days were now cooler, with earlier evenings and crisper mornings.

Autumn was approaching and would borrow darkness from the night and give it to the day.

"I saw Giant and Ade getting trimmed earlier. They're still coming," Slim said to Xavier and Fabian.

Ade, Giant and Slim resided in actual social houses (a much better living situation to residing on an estate) near the Jubilee clock in Harlesden, a town which was central to several gritty housing estates north, south and west of it - estates constantly at odds with one another.

People from the heart of Harlesden had a sort of impunity, though. They could move between the Stonebridge, St Raphael's, and Church End estates without having to explain their presence, unburdened by geographically imposed gang ties.

"What about Pauly Reggae? How come he ain't coming?" Fabian asked Slim.

"Don't know," Slim responded, rolling up Rizla paper.

"Yo! Tell me something. Why'd you call a White boy Pauly Reggae?" Fabian asked.

Slim licked the sticky seam of the Rizla and connected the two pieces.

"He likes Reggae, and his name is Paul," Slim responded in a monotone.

Xavier chuckled and shook his head.

"What?" Fabian responded to Xavier.

"Yo! Heads up. Paul and his madre." Xavier said.

Slim quickly stuffed the Rizla paper in his pocket and stood to attention.

Xavier reached into the car and reduced the volume of his brother's music. They stood as if a sergeant was about to inspect them.

Paul and his mother approached and stopped.

"Xavier, Fabian, Andre." Paul's mum said as she surveyed them.

"Good evening." They all said in unison.

"Good evening, is it? What did I just see in your hands, Andre, aka Slim?" Paul's mum asked.

Fabian wanted to laugh so badly. Slim opened the palms of his hands to her.

"Nothing," Slim responded.

"Nothing? Looked like the beginnings of something illegal to me," Paul's mum stated.

"No, we don't smoke weed or cigarettes, for that matter," Fabian announced.

Paul stood just behind his mother, covering his eyes with his hands, embarrassed by his mother and frustrated with Fabian and his loose tongue.

She scrutinised them from head to toe.

"Is it really? Interesting trousers, Xavier. Very colourful. They your pyjamas for the sleepover?" Paul's mum asked.

"Errrm. No." Xavier responded, panicking and scrambling for anything to respond with.

"Off-key, Mosh- sorry, I mean Moschino," Fabian said.

The boys burst out laughing. Paul's mum shook her head and smiled, wanting to laugh too, but couldn't let the bravado slip. She waited till they had finished.

"Where's your brother?" She asked Xavier.

Xavier pointed at his brother, who was standing outside his car, waiting to speak with Paul's mum.

She looked them over once more before moving around the vehicle.

Unlike Fabian, Xavier's brother was mature, level-headed and always had the right thing to say.

The boys all stood looking at each other and then at Fabian, who was sweating. No one dared to say a word. Paul's mum finished speaking and returned to them.

"Let me make something very clear. I want you to have fun, but I want you to be safe. You, hear me," Paul's mum stated.

"Loud and clear," Fabian responded.

Paul's mum shook her head at him, released a sigh, turned, hugged and kissed Paul on the cheek before she went back over to the estate, mumbling something about *off-key Mosh.*

Finally out of earshot, Paul turned to Fabian.

"You fool! Why do you have to reply to everything, man?" Paul questioned.

Fabian looked around at his friends, his face fashioned in disbelief.

"It's true, man. Your mouth's too big. Look how you nearly messed me up," Slim added.

"Yo! Look who's out and about," Xavier said, nodding towards Josephine, who passed Paul's mum and approached them.

"I bet that's P's plus one," Fabian joked.

Without a rebuttal, Slim and Xavier looked at Paul, their smiles slowly disappearing from their faces, and Paul began to grin.

"P. Tell me that ain't who you're bringing, bro," Xavier questioned.

"If it was?" Paul replied.

Xavier looked at Paul, his eyes wide, his mouth wider. Xavier grabbed Paul's arm and marched him away from the car.

"Are you mad?" Xavier asked.

"Why?" Paul responded.

Xavier blinked rapidly in disbelief.

"Blud, there is no way that girl can be seen with us in North West. Especially not in my brother's car," Xavier argued in a whisper.

"What's the big deal?" Paul asked.

They both regarded Josephine, stood several metres from the car, awaiting Paul.

"Her brother's a gangster, bro; how many times has he let it be known if anyone plays with his sister - It's that," Xavier stated, pulling an imaginary gun trigger on the 'That.'

The pair fell silent.

"I cannot believe you messed this up," Xavier stated.

Genuine disappointment was evident on Xavier's face. Paul could see the future father in him.

"Look, we gotta go. You can come in the car, but she can't, and that's it, bro," Xavier said, peering over at his big brother, who was tapping his watch.

Paul gazed thoughtfully.

"Alright. Well, what if we made our own way down?" Paul questioned.

"Don't know about that; I'll have to run it by my brother. I can tell you this: she cannot be seen leaving or coming back into the area with us. You, get me." Xavier replied.

"Look, give me the address. And we'll jump on the train."

Xavier appeared reluctant.

"Bro. Forget the party. You need to not be doing this. You're playing with fire," Xavier pleaded, his voice sounding worried.

Paul looked at him, and for the second time in their discussion, he noticed a seriousness in his friend's face that he had not seen before. A seriousness typically reserved for adults.

Paul glanced at Josephine - dressed in her finest. Sending her home was not an option. How could he be so cruel? Not only did he want her to go with him, but there was a degree of compulsion he appeared powerless to resist, a force driving him forward unabated.

"I hear you, bro... Look, I'll meet you there," Paul said, unable to find any other words for him.

Xavier shook his head.

"Up to you, mate," Xavier said, walking off to go and speak to his brother. Paul trailed after him. Fabian and Slim's eyes darted to and fro.

"What's the hold up?" Xavier's brother asked.

Xavier disclosed the details to him. Xavier's elder brother regarded Paul with displeasure, then addressed him.

"Can't lie P, this is bad business. I don't want her coming, but true say - she might take it offensively if I send her home. I'll have to let her - 'cause I don't need those sorts of problems with her brother. But hear this - she's one hundred per cent your responsibility, yeah." Xavier's brother said.

Paul was starting to feel the weight of his choices pressing upon him.

Xavier stating it was a bad idea was one thing, but his older brother had navigated the 'hood' his whole life without incident and was doing well. If Paul were to take advice from anyone beyond his mother, it would be him.

"Yeah," Paul responded.

Xavier's brother wrote the party's address on paper and handed it to him.

"Another thing. I got you safely to Fabian's house tonight. Yes. "Xavier's brother announced.

Paul gave a nod.

"No. Say it." Xavier's brother insisted, staring him dead in the eye.

Paul raised his hands in a gesture of acceptance.

"Okay, yes." Paul replied.

"Good. Now, I don't mind dropping you two back after, but you'll have to get out on Harrow Rd, and walk her back from there." Xavier's brother said.

Paul's plan was beginning to feel like a plan devised by a fifteen-year-old child—the best-case scenario at the forefront and 360 degrees all around, with not even a centimetre of consideration for any potential errors.

Not getting in the car was a significant stumbling block, and Paul knew he should have called it off, but his heart wasn't copying.

This would be the last party of a pretty "whack" summer, and he did not want to miss it.

Xavier's brother nodded towards Josephine.

"You better get going. But hear what. Stay on the back roads and make her walk a couple of paces up from you till you're out of the manor - try to avoid getting sighted with her." Xavier's brother advised.

Paul swallowed, his throat suddenly feeling remarkably dry. He nodded, turned, and slowly walked towards Josephine, who was playing with the corners of her cardigan, shifting her weight this way and that as if she wanted to pee.

She appeared as nervous as him.

'I can't come, can I?" Josephine asked.

Paul turned to look at his friends piling into the car. He found a smile for her.

"It's not that at all. It's just that Xavier's brother's worried about numbers in the car. Said the police are clamping down on overcrowding..." Paul lied.

"Is it really?" Josephine said as the car roared past them, her head tilted to indicate she wasn't buying his excuse.

"Swear," Paul replied.

The pair stood in awkward silence for a few seconds.

"Look, we'll go up on the train. Get a cab back." Paul revealed.

"You got that kind of money, yeah?" Josephine asked.

Paul had a small amount of cash but was relying on Xavier's brother's promise to drop them home afterwards.

"Course," Paul reassured.

In reality, Paul planned to take a train to Peckham, and then use his money to get a minicab from the train station to the address, in order to avoid getting lost.

✳✳✳✳✳

With Xavier's brother's warning ringing in Paul's mind, he was now concerned about reaching Willesden Junction train station without:

A. Being seen by anyone who could inform Josephine's brother that, in his unfortunate absence, Paul was openly frolicking with his younger sister on the verge of consummating their relationship - for that's how people operate; they see nothing untoward but relish drama, and if there was insufficient drama, they would take flamethrower to Rome and watch it burn.

The B. Was not being seen by anyone gang affiliated with Stonebridge - that would one hundred per cent take any opportunity they could to gain a stripe by shooting Jungle's little sister and company in retaliation for 'C10' gunning down three of theirs.

Paul suddenly felt very warm on that cool summer evening.

He had convinced himself that every car that passed was the last one he'd see before the big BANG! BANG! BANG!

He looked sideways at Josephine, oblivious to any possible threats, just skipping along, ignorant to any danger, chatting away, free as a bird.

"Why do you keep lagging like that?" Josephine asked, looking over her shoulder at Paul.

"Ha?" Paul responded, scanning their surroundings.

They were on St Mary's Road, fifteen minutes from Willesden Junction underground and rail station.

St Matthew's Church was to their right. Watching over them was a mahogany Jesus on a cross, hung over huge wooden doors.

The road ahead forked, separated by a parade of shops in the middle, then more homes. Bright orange-bricked terraced houses lined the street on both sides of the divide.

The road to their left of the fork would have taken them towards Willesden, and the road to the right, into the heart of Harlesden and, ultimately, towards the train station they needed - which was oddly called 'Willesden Junction', even though it wasn't actually in Willesden.

Paul's grandfather, his friend Rashida, and her younger sister lived to the right of the split.

Paul was deep in thought, formulating a backup strategy in the event they encountered any opposition.

He figured, if they were to be spotted, they could run to Rashida's or his grandfather's house. *But then, you'd bring heat to them?* His mind stated. *Yeah, but what other options would I hav-*

"Paaaul!" Josephine called, raising her voice. Paul leapt and turned to look at her.

"My goodness! What's up with you?" Josephine asked, having called his name three times, without a response.

She turned and began walking backwards to face him, stopped and placed her hand at the centre of his chest.

He stood at her arm's length.

"What're you doing?" Paul asked, looking in all directions.

"If you don't stop acting like I'm some sort of pariah, I'm going home. Walk with me properly or not at all," Josephine demanded.

Her accent was now 'proper', as he and his friends would have described it - her former privileged life commanding her speech. Paul lowered his head and raised his hands as if he were surrendering.

"I'm not stupid; by the way, I do know what you're doing," Josephine stated.

"Sorry?" Paul questioned.

" About sorry. Be honest. You got a girl you're trying to hide me from, haven't you?" Josephine elaborated.

Paul winced. *She's so sheltered it was painful*, he thought.

"Nah, man," Paul responded.

"Then what?"

"Trust me, it's nothing like that -I'm always cautious when I walk road."

"Cautious of? " Josephine questioned.

Paul shrugged.

"People innit... You know the situation with them and us. You gotta be watching at all times," Paul said, referring to the conflict between Church Rd and Stonebridge.

Josephine released a condescending chuckle.

This would be the first time she displayed a negative trait that Paul did not appreciate, and it would not be the last.

"You ain't no bad man, Paul. They aren't interested in you," Josephine stated.

It was Paul's turn to laugh now, far from amusement but out of sheer disbelief that someone could be so removed from their own circumstances. Oblivious to how their reality worked. He wasn't the reason they were in danger; she was.

Paul sighed.

"You're right. I'm being foolish," Paul said to appease.

"Okay, now that we've got that out of the way, let's get to this party, shall we?" she said, grabbing his hand, turning, and walking towards the train station.

When they walked out into Harlesden's centre from the back-roads, for some reason, the place was awash with police—tens of them walking and driving by.

A helicopter could be heard in the distance. The police's presence marked the absence of life-threatening danger.

Relief was not the word.

They walked past a parade of shops on their left—a mixture of hair products, bric-a-brac, Caribbean food and grocery stores. On the opposite side stood a McDonald's, mini casino, jewellery shop, and the world-renowned 'Mean Fiddler', a venue that welcomed legendary artists such as 'Van Morrison', 'Johnny Cash', 'Paul McCartney', and many more.

Connecting all roads and marking the town's centre was 'Queen Victoria's Jubilee clock', painted brilliant red with gold trimmings. It was old English craftsmanship woven into the tapestry of modern multicultural London.

Paul observed the clock as they passed it, reminded of the clock in his home, its hands striving to get away from each other.

- *Mad,* he thought.

As the Jubilee clock shrank in the distance, he glanced back once more, half-expecting to see its hands mirroring what he had observed at home, but he saw nothing untoward.

At Willesden Junction train station, the pair examined the train map, their fingers tracing rail lines, trying to find the best route to Peckham.

A station assistant approached, navigating through the throng of commuters entering and exiting via the gates.

She positioned herself behind them. Her uniform was a royal blue, with the Underground logo embroidered in red and outlined in white on her jacket pocket.

"Where are you trying to get to?" The assistant asked.

They turned and looked at the woman - she was Black, in her twenties, and slim.

"Peckham," Josephine stated.

"Peckham." The assistant repeated.

"Yeah," Paul added.

The woman's eyes shifted from Paul to Josephine, then returned to Paul. Paul and Josephine exchanged glances. The woman's behaviour was peculiar.

"Well. Peckham Rye is shut today, so you'll have to get a bus from Piccadilly Circus," the assistant stated.

"Okay," Paul said.

"Go to platform one downstairs. Catch the train to Piccadilly Circus, then get off. I don't know which bus to take, but you can ask one of my colleagues when you arrive," the assistant advised.

Paul offered her a nod.

"So Piccadilly Circus - and ask the staff there which bus to take," Josephine reiterated for clarity.

The woman smiled warmly.

"Yep."

They all stood still for a few seconds, just looking at each other until Paul initiated their departure.

"Thanks," Paul said, tugging Josephine's cardigan sleeve.

They resumed walking.

"yɛ ahwɛyie," the assistant whispered.

Josephine stopped and turned, her gaze fixed on the woman.

"Pardon?" Josephine asked.

Paul slowed to a halt and observed the pair.

The woman gave Josephine a warm smile.

"You two, be careful. Look after each other," the assistant replied.

The assistant's eyes glistened. She had the look of a mischievous child.

"Your Ghanian?" Josephine asked.

"Ye bishia beo," the assistant responded.

Josephine frowned.

"How did you know?" Josephine asked.

"Your," the assistant said, pulling her palms down both sides of her own cheeks. Then she winked and turned to face the line of commuters awaiting her assistance.

On the train, the pair sat silently beside each other, immersed in thought.

The train was partially full of young adults escaping the suburbs and heading into Central London, eager to dance repetitious lives away - a mix of Black and White working-class lads and lasses, drinking 'Thunderbirds', '20/20s' and 'Hooch'.

Josephine tapped Paul's leg to get his attention and had to raise her voice above the rowdy sound of weekend revellers and the groan of the train tracks beneath the train's wheels.

"Don't you think that woman was strange?"

Unable to hear her, Paul leaned in closer.

"Ha?" Paul responded.

"That woman, don't you think she was weird?" Josephine said.

"Oh, yeah. She was off-key. Cah -"

Before Paul could continue, the doors linking one train carriage to the next burst open on their left, and a file of elder Black teenagers came barrelling through.

They all had fresh trims—and were dressed in 'Iceberg', 'Moschino' shirts, 'Armani', 'Versace' jeans, and 'Shelly's' loafers. 'Joop' and 'Coolwater' fragrances trailed them as they passed— *Gyalis (90s slang for Ladies' men) and Earnertons (90s slang for high earners)*, as Paul and his friends would have labelled them.

The guys eyed everyone as they advanced. Passengers aboard the train appeared concerned.

'Gyalis' or 'Earnertons' were popular guys from the area, but weren't really involved in any criminal activity.

They simply enjoyed earning money, socialising, looking good, and ultimately attracting women - one or two may have teetered on the boundary between street life and civilian life, but for the most part, they were in education, holding 9-to-5 jobs, aspiring footballers or athletes who happened to reside in a deprived area.

The entire carriage remained silent until the guys entered the next railcar.

Josephine observed them, then redirected her gaze to Paul. Paul expected her to seem concerned; instead, she appeared in awe.

"You know them?" Josephine asked, thumbing in their direction.

"One or two of their faces, they're older. From around the way." Paul responded.

If Black people could blush, Paul was confident Josephine would have been bright red.

The interconnecting carriage door the youths had passed through swung back and forth, clanging until a man got up and closed it.

"Why?" Paul asked.

She looked at Paul with a grin.

"No reason," Josephine replied.

Paul frowned, feeling a hint of jealousy.

"Anyway! It was Piccadilly Circus, right?" Paul questioned.

"Yep! Piccadilly," Josephine said.

Paul glanced up at the train map across from them, only visible intermittently between the swaying of a couple standing before them holding the handrail above.

They passed Kilburn Park, Paddington, Marylebone and Baker St.

As additional passengers boarded, the train grew crowded.

With the crowd of people obstructing their view, Josephine and Paul struggled to see the map and could only make out the 'Circus' segment of Oxford or Piccadilly Circus upon it.

"Does that say Oxford Circus or Piccadilly next?" Paul asked Josephine.

"Not sure. Hold on," Josephine said, standing to get a better look.

The only problem was that she was too short to see over the row of human heads and limbs. Before she realised, the train had stopped, and the herd of people within commenced exiting, sweeping her off the carriage with them.

Paul leapt up from his seat and seized Josephine's outstretched arm.

"Aye, yo!" Paul shouted, trying his best to grab hold of her.

Powerless to prevent her being pushed out with the crowd's momentum, they both found themselves on the platform, facing a torrent of commuters rushing past one another onto the platform in a frenzy.

When the crowd dispersed, the train doors had closed. The train commenced its departure.

"Wow! That was mad," Paul said.

Josephine giggled.

"This your first time on the Tube?" She asked.

"Nah. But every time I've come on, I've been with my school, my mum or them lot. You?" Paul replied.

"Loads. Before my dad died, we used to go on trips to Central all the time," she said.

"We're at the wrong station, by the way; this is Oxford Circus," Josephine added, looking at the station name on the wall opposite them.

Josephine looked up at the information board to check the time of the next train.

The display unit was black, rectangular and suspended from the ceiling. A single red digital line ran across the middle of its screen where the time for the next train should have been.

Advertisement posters took the shape of the cylindrical station walls.

The floor tiles were beige brown, with two thick raised yellow lines on a bed of raised grooves—used to signify to people and the visually impaired that they were approaching the platform's edge.

The air smelt of dirty soot and charred train brake pads.

They began walking towards a station assistant at the far end to ask them when the next train would arrive.

"It must be weird for you," Paul said.

"How do you mean?" Josephine replied.

"Like…You used to be kinda rich, and now you're with us. " Paul continued.

She gazed ahead.

"I try not to think about it." She responded.

They proceeded in silence for a brief period.

"Hope I haven't -" Paul began.

"Really, it's fine," Josephine said, cutting Paul.

The platform assistant was conversing back and forth over a crackly walkie-talkie.

"Okay, copy." The platform assistant said, then looked down at the pair.

"Sorry, guys. The Bakerloo line has been suspended due to an incident at Queens Park. We await further information," the platform assistant stated.

He relayed the information over the tannoy, and commuters on the platform began making their way towards him and the exits.

"We have to get to Piccadilly Circus," Josephine informed him.

"Well, you can wait and see what happens here. It could be five minutes or five hours. Or you could enjoy the fine summer evening with a stroll." The platform assistant replied.

The pair exchanged glances, seeking a decision from each other.

"Shall we?" Paul asked.

Josephine shrugged.

"Good choice. So leave the station, take a left down Regents Street, and stay straight. Go past the big screens on Leicester Square, and Piccadilly will be directly ahead of you. Twenty minutes tops," the platform assistant instructed and insured.

"Thanks," Josephine replied.

They exited the station.

Outside, in the fading daylight of the West End's exclusive shopping district, it felt as though they had been delivered into the land of the living on steroids—everything was so fast-paced.

People of diverse backgrounds scurry about, eager to return home from office and retail jobs, while others were keen to socialise with the arriving crowds, gallivanting and seeking the start of a great night out.

The atmosphere was nothing less than electric. Vendors sold food, drinks, drugs, tickets for raves, counterfeit aftershaves, and an assortment of goods from makeshift tables tucked away in nooks and side streets.

The pavements there are wider than anywhere else in London—big industrial concrete slabs strong enough to cope with Oxford Street's enormous daily footfall.

The smell of car exhausts, fried onions, sausages, and burgers from vendors hung thick in the air.

All the major brands had their flagship stores there. 'Madhouse', 'Gap', 'HMV', 'McDonald's', 'DKNY', 'Ralph Lauren' and more. Their store signs compete to outshine one another.

London's iconic black cabs and red route masters hummed up and down the roads.

Josephine and Paul enjoyed the sounds humans make when carefree and under the influence of freedom.

Paul's housing estate - his cradle, coffin, and the people in and around it began to feel insignificant regarding their world relevance. With an array of notable companies calling the West End home 'British Airways', 'Coca-Cola', 'Disney', 'BFI',

'Sony' and a flurry of Fortune 500 businesses, they now walked among movers and shakers, giants that contributed to the carving, direction and trajectory of fashion, music, food, entertainment and life globally.

The throng of people Paul and Josephine had to navigate around and through was immense—surging and spilling off the pavement.

They passed huge shop fronts on either side of Regents Street.

Black cabs with their small yellow lights atop whizzed up and down the road, pulling up and over at intervals to pick up or set down passengers.

Down the centre of the road was a lengthy concrete island that opened in sections to allow people to cross from one side to the other. Huge Union Jacks were suspended above the island from lampposts.

Paul stopped at 'Russell and Bromley' and pointed at the price of a pair of blue suede loafers.

"Three bills for that?" Paul said.

Josephine's eyes widened - then she looked across at a pair of women's black patent high heels.

"Look. What about those?"

"Rah! Three hundred and fifty pounds, you know!" Paul responded.

"That's one month's rent," Josephine stated.

Paul looked down at their trainers—both wearing worn-in Rebook classics. Their pairs were worth sixty pounds in total, sixty pounds that their parents probably had to scrimp and scrape to make.

A well-dressed, dapper man walked up to the glass on the other side of the shoe display, looking down his nose at Paul and Josephine. He began to adjust and dust down the shoes.

Paul sniggered and shook his head.

"Come, let's go," Josephine said.

"Nah, let's go in for a bit," Paul said, walking towards the shop door, in a gesture of protest.

The man walked with him on the other side of the glass and mouthed 'Closed'. Paul tried the handle anyway.

The man repeated, 'Closed!' but louder. Paul cut him a look, and the man grinned.

Josephine tutted.

"Let's go; remember, we have a party to get to," Josephine said, pulling Paul's arm.

"People like that pee me off," Paul said as they walked away.

"Why let it get to you?" Josephine asked.

"What? You couldn't see how he was eyeing us up?" Paul responded.

"Man's a racist." Paul continued.

"You can't say that from a look."

Paul shook his head.

"You do know you are Black, right?" Paul asked.

"Daaah!" Josephine responded.

"Then you should know White people are racist against us," Paul stated as if it was a given.

Josephine laughed.

"That's ridiculous. My father had many White friends, and none of them were racist. How many times has someone been racist towards you?" Josephine asked.

Paul had to think—and think some more. Besides the last remnant of a fleeting Irish community, Harlesden in the 90s was a predominantly Caribbean area, and Paul hardly knew any White people except

Pauly Reggae, Tom, and Jean, Melissa's best friend, none of whom he considered White.

His perception of White people had been shaped by his dealings with the police in his area, television, and overheard conversations between his uncles, aunts, and family friends, who would criticise the government, their managers, and work colleagues, with racism being a common theme.

"I was only ten minutes late, you know, and the man's telling me he thinks I may have a problem with timekeeping. You know what his problem is, don't you?" Uncle Colin would rant.

"Yep." Paul's mum would say, nodding in agreement.

"Racism!" They'd say in unison.

"Bout, I can't bring my food into the office 'cause it's too spicy for Sandra, blasted racists! dem fi gah suck dem -" Aunt Pearl would begin.

"Peeeearl! Language!" Paul's mum would interject.

"These Tories are BNP in suits!" Uncle Juicy used to say in any given situation.

Josephine and Paul slowed their pace at a crossing.

"See, if you have to think about it, it proves you wrong."

"Yeah, whatever," Paul responded.

It was the darker part of dusk now.

As they rounded the corner to exit Regent's Street into Leicester Square, their eyes widened.

Colossal electronic advertisement screens were mounted around the corner of the building, projecting vibrant ideas for purchase in the fading daylight.

The screens were so bright it was as if a star had fallen to earth and shattered into squares. 'Coca-Cola',

'Vogue', 'Ford', 'McDonald's', and other ads ran in a loop.

Paul stood in awe. Until that moment, the freight train, with its twinkling yellow side lights and neon red rears, was the most magnificent display of human innovation he had observed in person.

The screens resembled something from *Back to the Future 2,* he contemplated.

Being in the West End was proving more exciting than any house party could be.

Paul could have stood there all night, walked around the area until dawn, and remained until dusk, and was certain he would not have been disappointed.

"You've never seen these?" Josephine asked, pointing at the screens.

Paul was slow to respond - lost in contemplation.

"Paul." Josephine continued.

"Not in the evening," Paul murmured.

Josephine smiled.

"Wait till you see Chinatown."

"Chinatown?" Paul repeated.

"Yep. Let's go."

Josephine tugged his arm, and they proceeded towards Piccadilly Circus tube station.

The crowds grew denser, with no rhyme or reason to the flow of people. They approached a crossing. Paul checked to his right for approaching vehicles, and when he turned back to look for Josephine, in her place, was a stream of people walking to and fro across the street.

Paul stepped into the middle of the road and found himself jostled and nudged by pedestrians from both directions as he spun around, searching for Josephine.

Before he realised, the crowd had dispersed, and he was standing with two sets of car headlights approaching him.

A man darted out and pulled Paul to safety by the arm.

Everyone looked over at Paul, tutting and murmuring.

The man walked Paul away from the crossing to the front of a 'Boots' store under the advertising screens. Paul's chest was pounding.

"Are you trying to kill yourself or what? What were you thinking?" The man asked Paul.

"Looking for a girl, I mean, my friend who's a girl," Paul responded.

The man looked perplexed.

"Your girlfriend?"

"Nah, I, I uh, I mean -"

"It doesn't matter. You need to be careful, mate. You only get one life." The man responded, placing his hand on Paul's shoulder and patting his side. The man smiled at Paul.

His left eye was completely white, and he was missing teeth. He appeared to be on his ninth life.

"I need to go," the man said, gesturing towards a woman who didn't appear much better than him.

"Okay, thanks, yeah," Paul said.

The man didn't respond.

Paul continued towards Leicester Square in search of Josephine, slowly walking up Coventry Street, looking down and in all side roads, alleys, and shops to locate her.

He approached and stood by a McDonald's on a corner. He surveyed the crowd as they shimmered down the illuminated walkway and nearly forgot his purpose there.

He had never witnessed such diversity of people or heard so many languages spoken at the same time.

It was as though every nation had sent a representative to London. Paul began to realise that the world beyond 'NW10' was something to marvel at; and he wanted to be a part of it.

Four teenagers emerged from the crowd and positioned themselves directly in front of Paul.

One of them lit a cigarette, took a puff, and passed it to his companion on his left.

"What we doing tonight?" One of them asked the rest.

"Don't know."One of them responded.

"Back to the manor?" another suggested.

"Nah, man. Bridge is dead. Too much Feds about."

Paul's eyes widened upon hearing 'Bridge' and he decided to move before he was identified, even if by the slimmest of chances.

Paul slipped off to their right, but before he was beyond earshot, he heard one of them remark.

"Yo, ain't that Jungle's sister?"

Paul turned quickly and saw Josephine looking lost in the crowd just in front of McDonald's.

"Yeah, that's her."

"Come," one of the boys instructed the rest, reaching under his T-shirt by his waist, where he produced a small flick knife that he concealed down by his side.

The boys began moving through the crowd in single file.

Josephine was on the move once more, heading back towards Piccadilly. Paul began running towards her, pushing through and shoving people aside.

He grabbed the fabric of her cardigan shoulder and tugged her forward.

"Run!" Paul shouted.

Josephine seized his hand and flung it off.

"What the bloody hell do you think you're doing!? Where have you been!?"

"I'll explain in a minute! Run!" Paul said, grabbing her wrist and pulling her towards him.

"No! What's this all about?"

Paul observed the boys advancing aggressively through the crowd, their faces focused on their target.

"Josephine! If you don't move, you're gonna get stabbed!" Paul shouted, pointing at the advancing boys - his voice in a frenzied state.

She looked at Paul, her mouth forming an 'O', her eyes wide. She turned and saw them, their angry brown faces distinct amidst the sea of mostly white ones.

They set off, Paul shoving individuals left, right and centre to clear their path.

Once free of the crowd, they turned down a side street, running at full pace.

They took a left turn, then a right.

Josephine began to slow, then stopped, bending over, clutching both knees and panting heavily. Paul glanced back at her, stopped and hurried back.

"Ha..Ha..Who were they?" Josephine asked.

Paul's heart was racing. He placed his hands on his waist and leaned back to regain his breath.

"I do-hah-do-hah-don't.. don't know...They had a knife. They ta-ha-ta-ha talked about your brother." Paul said, gasping for air.

Josephine suddenly screamed, her eyes widened, brimming with dread; her hands came to her mouth and covered it whilst stumbling backwards, almost tripping over herself.

Paul turned, coming face-to-face with one of the boys who were chasing them.

The guy thrust his arm forward towards Paul's abdomen. Paul grabbed the guy's wrist with both hands, holding it firmly away from himself.

Paul looked him in the eye.

"Do.. Don't…" Paul mumbled, but when he looked down, it was too late - the guy no longer held the knife. Instead; the knife's brown handle stuck out of Paul's stomach.

Paul released the guy's wrist, and the guy took two steps back, appearing as surprised as Paul. Paul gripped the knife handle with one hand.

"Wh..Wh…Why?" Paul mumbled.

"Someone call an ambulance!" Paul heard Josephine scream at his rear.

Paul stumbled forward towards the guy.

"Whhh..Why?" Paul murmured, a single tear rolled down his face.

He thought of his mother watching her Saturday evening television programmes, unaware that her son could be drawing his final breaths on the squalid streets of Soho, unaware that Paul may never again pass through her front door.

"Forever fifteen", they would say of him. They would lay flowers and candles at his block and perhaps write his name somewhere.

He thought of his little brother and how they would never get to watch the beginning and end of 'RoboCop' again; or play 'Super Mario' together. But what really saddened him most, was that he would never hear his little brother's laugh ever again.

The thoughts wrapped him in sorrow.

His assailant's expression was peculiar. If Paul was not mistaken, he appeared mortified. It was as if he wished to say sorry, but he did not; instead, the boy turned and commenced sprinting towards his friends; upon reaching them, they all scattered.

Paul fell back into Josephine's arms as she screamed for help.

Then things became blurred, gradually fading to black and growing increasingly serene, until total silence prevailed. Paul's heart beat slowed, then stopped.

The Heavens

It is daytime. This place is the most breathtaking summer's day one could envisage. Golden stars twinkle through the sunlit clouds above. Everything is whiter than white; the colour of the grass, plants and trees is saturated to the utmost.

Birds sing, and bees hum and attend to red, purple and yellow roses.

Paul is immersed in a bed of lush green grass.

The grass smells divine.

A profound sense of peace envelops him; he could lie there for eternity.

Hovering above and gazing down upon him are two Moirai (the angels of human fate), one is Black (Hemsut) and one is White (Istustaya).

Their bodies are draped in silken-golden sarongs, adorned with every beautiful gemstone God has bestowed upon the earth.

Hemsut holds a string throbbing with golden light in one hand and a pair of glowing scissors in the other.

Istustaya holds a large brown book labelled 'Deja vu'.

They both examine Paul, scanning him from head to toe.

Istustaya gazed skywards and squinted in deep thought.

"Hmmm..He is different," Istustaya whispered.

"Nonsense!" Hemsut barked.

"Not at all!" Istustaya responded.

"If his time is up! It's up!" Hemsut argued.

"After three thousand years of doing this, you still want to rush."

"Look. He is our final allocation; we cut him and we have fulfilled Father's quota. Then we get to rest," Hemsut said.

"I understand that, but you have your job, and I mine. We must proceed properly. Something in the pages tells me he has..." Istustaya said as she squinted, then shook her head gently from side to side.

"Let me go to the -," Istustaya continued.

"Book! Always the book! Look where it got you with Hit -"

"Don't you - daaare mention that name. He was only five then, and I felt he was destined for something off the scale, which he was, but not how I envisioned it. Besides, there was a mix-up, he didn't belong to us, but to..." Istustaya said, pointing down.

"Anyhow!" Istustaya shouted.

Istustaya opened the book (Deja vu) and placed her finger on Paul's entry, scanning the text.

"See, look here! He fits the criteria for a second chance perfectly! Paul K Hawk. Sins are near zero, and look where he's coming from - he could have easily been tempted into wicked things. I assure you, this one is strong, a leader even - destined for a greater purpose. He shall guide many to the Father. "

Silence falls between the Moirai.

Hemsut scrutinised him once more.

"Hmmm." Hemsut sounded.

"You know I'm right - he is worthy of the pass. Allow him back, but give him intuition when they turn the corner- Oh, and the girl..."

"Josephine?" Hemsut said.

"Yes," Istustaya responded, pointing her fingers together at the tips.

"Guide them," Hemsut said, her eyes wide.

Hemsut's eyes sparkle.

"Oh, you think it could be.."

Istustaya nodded with her sister.

"Yep."

"Alright, alright, alright, I love a good love story—but I warn you, if he comes back—" Hemsut opened and closed the pair of glowing scissors before placing Paul's heartstring back into her yarn.

The women looked down upon Paul and murmured spiritual words. Then Istustaya slammed the book shut, and suddenly, the white became black, and Paul was free-falling back to earth, his heart began to beat again.

Back to life - Back to reality

Paul's heart was racing. He placed his hands on his waist and leaned back to regain his breath.

"I do-hah-do-hah-don't.. don't know...They had a knife. They ta-ha-ta-ha talked about your brother." Paul said, gasping for air.

Josephine suddenly screamed, her eyes widened, brimming with dread; her hands came to her mouth and covered it whilst stumbling backwards, almost tripping over herself.

Paul turned, coming face-to-face with one of the boys who were chasing them.

Paul jumped to the boy's left, narrowly missing the oncoming blade—then to his right, making his attacker miss again.

Paul leant back and launched a kick to the centre of the boy's chest, sending him flying; his knife thrown into the air.

The rest of the boys began shouting, screaming and sprinting towards their fallen friend.

Before the boy could gather himself, Paul turned on his heel, pushed Josephine, and the pair ran again.

"This way!" Paul shouted.

The pair took another corner, pushing further into the back streets of Soho.

Paul looked over his shoulder, and the boys were still chasing.

"Right! Right!" Paul screamed at Josephine, hoping they would double back onto themselves and get back to the main strip, confident that their pursuers would not be so foolish as to attack them in front of hundreds of witnesses.

Around the corner, Paul and Josephine encountered the entrance to a sixty-metre-long alleyway.

Josephine attempted to run back out, but the boys were there, walking now, closing in on their position.

Josephine and Paul turned and ran further down to the end of the alley. At the end, they encountered an eight-foot wall.

Josephine looked at Paul, then back at the boys, their blades glistening under the street lights. Paul knelt down.

"I'll boost you, go up, get help!" Paul instructed.

"No way, I'm not leaving you," Josephine responded.

"Yo! Times up, my yout!" One of the boys screamed, swooshing his knife through the air.

Paul looked at him, then back at Josephine, and gulped.

"I'll be alright; come on, go!" Paul shouted.

Josephine's eyelids fluttered, tears streaming between her lashes and down her face as she placed her foot on his knee.

Paul used all his strength to push her up onto the wall.

Once atop, Josephine knelt on the bricks, one hand extended to Paul, the other used to steady herself.

One of the boys broke away from the group and charged.

"Take my hand!" Josephine screamed.

Paul watched the boy approaching, running at a sprint.

"Paul! Take my hand now, damn it!" Josephine screamed.

Paul grabbed her arm, and Josephine clutched him; she pulled upwards and backwards, her nails embedding into his flesh as she clung to him; Paul gained just enough leverage to grip the top of the wall and hoist himself up in time.

The pair gazed down at the boy, then at the others arriving, all breathing heavily.

The boy who had attempted to stab Paul tried to leap up, and Paul delivered a kick to his head.

The boy fell back to the ground, clutching his head and making high-pitched sounds of agony.

"Watch when we catch you," one of the boys growled, pulling his finger across his neck.

"You two, go round to the other side! We'll wait here," one of the boys instructed, whilst the boy who got kicked hopped about in agony.

Paul burst out laughing. Josephine looked at Paul as if he were insane.

"You think this is funny, yeah? Watch!" one of the boys shouted.

Paul put a finger to his lips to shush him. Josephine looked down on the other side of the wall. The building's fire escape door was ajar. The faint sound of music could be heard emanating from within.

Josephine tapped Paul's arm and gestured towards the open door with a nod.

"Your brother's gonna hold uh hot one." The boy threatened.

"Just shut up!" Josephine screamed.

"Come," Paul said before he hung on the other side of the wall, dropped down, and moved towards the open door.

"Your bro's gonna get wet up! And as soon as five O move off your block, we're coming to your madres!" the boy threatened.

Josephine stared down at him. She gathered saliva and spat; the boy evaded it.

"Nice try!" The boy shouted in response.

"I think he's cracked my skull! My chest and my skull! I need to go hospital!" The boy Paul kicked protested.

"Shut up! You're making us look mad out here!" The boy responded to his wounded friend.

"Joe, come on!" Paul shouted from the ground.

Josephine dangled her legs from the wall, and Paul aided her descent.

The two other boys eventually emerged at the far end of the alleyway and began running towards them.

Josephine and Paul slipped through the crack in the fire escape door and closed it.

From outside, the door sprang to life with banging, kicking and shouting. Josephine looked worried; Paul pointed down at the door's handlebar.

"Only opens from inside," Paul said.

"Oh," Josephine responded.

"Come," Paul instructed.

They walked the gloomy passageway in search of the music. Aged, dirty light fixtures protruded and adorned the black corridor walls. The bulbs emitted a yellowing, faint light, struggling to survive, crackling and flickering on and off, their glow barely escaping the blackness of the walls.

The pair could barely see a foot in front.

The corridor guided them straight.

They pressed on into the building's depths.

Josephine glanced back and forth, weighing advance and retreat.

They trailed their fingers along the stone corridor wall to assist their senses.

The place reeked of cigarettes, stale beer and potpourri.

"What do you think this place is?" Josephine whispered.

Paul slowed his pace.

"Don't know. Has to be a nightclub, right. Just gotta work out how to reach the dance floor, then we can find someone to call the police." Paul reasoned.

The corridor veered left, and the sound of music grew more pronounced.

A slow, melodic piece of jazz.

A set of black cast iron stairs confronts them leading up to a set of closed double doors. Light emanates from the door's seams, slowly changing colour - from pink to yellow, yellow to green and blue.

They looked up the stairs in silence, and then Paul took the first step, followed by another and more, until he reached the peak—with Josephine close behind.

He placed both hands upon the massive wooden doors.

A green and white fire exit sign is illuminated overhead.

Paul turned and gave Josephine a look which said 'shall I open them', she nodded. With that, he pushed against both doors; they did not open easily, but with a little more effort, they gave way.

They are greeted by a vast, empty dance floor, with disco lights rolling and twirling slowly above, changing direction and colour sporadically.

Tables and chairs are arranged around the outer perimeter of the dance floor.

A raised DJ booth occupies the centre of the room. To their right stands a long bar with drinks and finger food displayed on the wall behind.

A White man, with his back to them, is sitting at the bar. His head is enveloped in a haze of cigarette smoke.

They stand just outside the room, feeling apprehensive about entering.

The man raised his hand, which held a remote control. He pointed the remote towards the DJ booth, and the music gradually became softer and softer until it was barely audible.

He lowered his arm.

"To the damn second," the man said before he began to laugh, shaking his head.

Smoke drifts above him in a rough circle, like a smouldering halo.

Paul and Josephine exchanged a concerned look.

"Paul K Hawk, Josephine Appiah, welcome," the man said before taking another drag of the cigarette, releasing more smoke.

Paul stared at the man's back. Josephine looked back down the steps into the darkness below, and a shiver ran down her spine.

"How do you know our names?" Paul asked.

The man paused for several seconds, then slowly rotated in the bar chair and fixed them with a penetrating gaze.

"Do you know this place normally takes at least two thousand pounds on a night like this? I closed it just for you two," the man replied.

Paul considered the statement, but the boys outside attempting to kill them was a more pressing concern.

"I hear that…But could you get the police? Some guys are chasing us with knives." Paul said.

"We're sorry for trespassing, but we really need your help," Josephine added.

The man chuckled.

"You asked how I knew your names right? I mean, if a stranger knew mine, I would want answers," the man said.

Paul and Josephine did not respond but regarded him, contemplating the situation.

The man observed them for five seconds, his facial expression a blend of astonishment and amusement.

"Don't you want to know how I knew you'd be here?" the man asked.

Paul attempted to respond, but the man spoke over him.

"Look at this," the man said, sliding an envelope onto the counter.

He tapped the letter as he spoke.

"So five years ago, I began renovating my house. An electrician was lifting floorboards to run new cables. He got to work in my room, and from under where my bed was, he pulled this letter out from under the floor and handed it to me. My name on it, and everything."

The man chuckled to himself, shaking his head from side to side.

"Thought he was pulling some kind of joke. Anyway. I checked with my wife, brother and anyone I have ever had around; ha! I even asked the postman if he knew anything about it. None of them did. Needless to say, uncovering how it had got there became somewhat of an obsession, to put it mildly." The man said.

The man paused, looked above their heads and then down at their feet.

"It consumed me. Even when I claimed it didn't, it did. I began investigating the history of the house, its previous owners and the surrounding area."

The man paused once more, then reached into the breast pocket of his shirt and withdrew a packet of cigarettes, offering the open box - three brown cigarette butts were pressed against one another.

"No, thank you," Josephine said.

He presented the packet to Paul, and Paul waved him off.

"Suit yourself." the man responded.

The man pulled one out, placed it between his teeth, brought his trembling hand to his lips, and lit it with a lighter.

He took a deep drag and continued talking, releasing smoke through his nose and the corners of his mouth.

"You see, everyone said to forget about it, to let it go, that it was a coincidence. But even when I wished to move on with my life, the letter and today's date lingered in the corner of my mind, refusing to leave, telling me that I could dismiss it and attribute it to any of the excuses I have been provided with by some of the most accomplished charlatans and spiritual men money could procure over the last five years, yet I knew this was no mere coincidence. Nope!" He said, tapping the letter.

"Paulette and Cuthbert Hawk," he suddenly pronounced, raising his voice.

He looked at Paul as if to say, "Tah-dah!" Paul stared back, his eyes slowly moving around the man's face.

"My grandparents," Paul stated, touching his collarbone and stepping forward, both eyes in a squint.

"I know—they owned my house until they sold it in 1972 to Mr and Mrs Singh. Nineteen Robin Hood Way," the man said, his eyes wide now, focused on a point beyond Josephine and Paul.

"What does it say?" Josephine interjected.

They both looked at her, then Paul at him for the answer.

The man nodded, placed the cigarette in an ashtray and cleared his throat.

"Dear Jason King, that's me. On Saturday, the 28th of August 1998, at 19:30, please leave the fire escape door of the 'Turbine' open to let Paul K Hawk and Josephine Appiah in. 'The Father' would really appreciate it. Signed Jacob Hawk. 1972." Jason read.

"What!" Paul barked.

Jason nodded and began to smile from ear to ear.

"I know, right…"

Paul turned to Josephine.

"Jacob is my dad," Paul said.

"Okay. But who's the Father?" Josephine asked, thinking the letter could somehow be referring to her father.

Jason smiled and pointed towards the ceiling.

"I've been watching you two for years - waiting for this to play out! Waiting for my part. Your comings and goings from school to chilling in the park with Rich and the rest. Both your mother's lives, friends and family - sadly, your brother Josephine, I know everything about you. Having the financial resources I have made it easy." Jason stated.

They both looked like rabbits in big beams.

'You've been watching us?" Paul questioned.

"Hey, when you personally receive a letter from the past about the future, and you look into it, and the characters are real - trust me, you pull out all the stops. Let's say I've spent a fortune finding you and keeping watch."

"What!? I mean, I don't understand this; what's happening?" Josephine asked.

Paul shook his head.

"Jacob Hawk is my father. How could he have known? I wasn't even..."

Jason shook his head. The disco lights danced on top of him and the bar, with red, yellow, purple and green spots appearing and vanishing with each twist and turn.

"Don't even try to get it, it'll drive you nuts. Five years I've been waiting for this night. You have no idea how happy I am that you're here. How relieved I am that I'm not crazy. You know I lost my wife over this? I lost friends and virtually all of my family. My wife got up one day and said I loved the letter more than I loved her; she was right. I've had money and status from birth, yet I have never had a purpose, nor believed in anything beyond my wealth. But this..this gave me something beyond my limitless finances, something I couldn't explain or buy an answer for, this was simply…Simply divine." Jason said.

Paul and Josephine observed Jason kiss a crucifix hung around his neck.

"The letter wasn't the only thing in the envelope. I think these are also meant for you," Jason said, rummaging around in his trouser pockets.

He produced a brown leather wallet, extracted two golden travel cards, and positioned them on the bar.

"Here," Jason said to them.

He then cleared his throat.

"I think that's it from me. Paul, Josephine, I express gratitude to the Lord for allowing me to be a part of whatever you are a part of; this divine situation bestowed upon me faith and belief in the beyond. Saved me from a meaningless life." Jason stated.

With that, Jason stood up from his stool.

"I'll give you guys fifteen minutes to process what I've had five years to." Jason said.

He then glanced upwards at a small screen above the bar that displayed a CCTV image of his three doormen gesticulating with the Stonebridge boys outside.

"I'll get security to get rid of them. Give you enough time to get away. Go out the back. Leave the rest to me," Jason said.

"Can't you just call us a cab?" Josephine asked.

Jason sucked on his lower lip and regarded her.

"I don't think this works like that; you got those tickets for a reason; I don't want to disturb whatever is planned for you. I don't think it would be wise. I wouldn't have wanted anyone to interfere with my blessing," Jason said, walking towards the exit.

He departed, leaving Josephine and Paul standing in silence absorbing the moment.

"What just happened?" Josephine asked the room, disco lights frantically revolving across the walls and over an empty dance floor.

"I don't know, but this night is getting crazier by the second. Them man will never believe this," Paul said.

Paul approached the counter, retrieved both tickets, and analysed them.

The tickets were more rigid than the typical cardboard variety one would obtain from the machine. Upon closer inspection, it became evident they were composed of a thick, metallic/golden material.

The tickets read 'valid from: *Kensal Rise* and the destination: *The Park*,' but the strangest thing about them was the time constantly changing, fading between dawn and night hours.

"Yo! Come see this," Paul said.

Josephine approached him and scrutinised the tickets.

"Oh my God, How?" Josephine said, questioning the morphing time.

"What does it mean destination The Park?" Josephine questioned.

Paul shrugged.

"Let's get out of here. My mind's hurting," Paul stated.

He handed Josephine a ticket, and she placed it in her cardigan pocket. Paul slipped his ticket into his jeans pocket.

They exited through the door, by which they had entered and descended the staircase.

Paul cautiously peered out of the exit door, scanning left and right to ensure the area was clear. He slipped outside and checked again before telling Josephine to follow.

Paul gestured towards the wall they had scaled earlier.

"We should go back up and walk down to distance ourselves from here," Paul proposed.

Josephine nodded in agreement.

They aided one another back up and surveyed the length of the wall before them.

They walked single-file under a giant yellow moon—the heavens adorned with stars. They passed the backs of 'Soho' restaurants, nightclubs and wine bars.

Muffled music filled the air, and the aroma of food and refuse from the bins below assailed them as they traversed the wall at the rear of establishments in full Saturday swing.

"Here should be enough," Josephine said.

Paul slowed to a stop and turned to confront her.

"You reckon?" Paul responded.

"Yeah, we can climb down into this yard, then go over that wall, and I think we'll be back out onto the street," Josephine suggested.

Paul remained silent for a moment. He inhaled, then spoke.

"Can I tell you something?" Paul asked.

Josephine was uncertain whether she was prepared to hear anything else after Jason's bizarre reveal.

"I err. I. I suppose so," Josephine replied reluctantly.

"Cool…In my house, I have this clock, yeah. Me and my brother smashed it, and it hasn't worked for at least a year. But when I was leaving to come out tonight, I saw it ticking, but the hands were going mad! When I went to show my mum, it was back to being broken again." Paul said.

Josephine licked her dry lips.

"Serious. That's weird. Can I tell you something?" She replied.

"Course," Paul responded.

"Well, before I left out, my reflection wasn't mine; I mean, it was mine, but it was strange, moving a second behind my movement," Josephine replied.

Below where they stood on the wall was the rear of a bar/restaurant, which had massive industrial bins, crates, supplies and rodents around the floor beneath.

"Why didn't you say this earlier?" Paul asked.

Josephine shrugged.

"I don't know. Why didn't you?" She responded.

Paul looked above her head towards the direction from which they had just come.

"To be honest. I was kinda shook," Paul replied, dipping his head.

Josephine grasped his hand.

"So was I," Josephine said.

"Oi! What you doing up there?!" A man dressed in chef's regalia bellowed from the restaurant's rear entrance.

The pair looked at him. But before they could react, an object came hurtling from the chef's direction - fast, striking Paul directly in the face, causing him to lose his balance. Paul clung to Josephine in a desperate attempt to remain upright, but it was too late; he had already lost his balance and was now falling, taking Josephine with him.

They fell in slow motion through a pane of glass in the roof of an outbuilding on the opposite side of the wall, both screaming at the top of their lungs. Their eyes closed, anticipating impact, yet the landing was gentle, as if they had fallen onto a haystack.

Their eyes sprang open, scanning their surroundings.

It was daytime, and they were on a bed in a bedroom.

The room was bright, painted in a mint green shade. A window above them cast a bar of light across their faces. Paul and Josephine surveyed the room. Paul placed both palms against his face and patted, checking for damage.

"Where are we?" Josephine murmured.

The sound of commotion emanated from the stairs beyond the closed door, accompanied by a muffled, deep voice demanding their attention.

The room door handle turned, and Paul and Josephine's eyes widened in anticipation of who would enter and find them on their bed.

The door opened, and Paul's father - Jacob - entered, but it was not Paul's dad in their present. It was Paul's dad at eighteen.

Jacob glanced in their direction but then turned away, as if they were not present. Jacob went to the drawers, pulled them open, grabbed his underwear, and stuffed them into a black bin liner whilst grumbling.

Paul began to edge himself off the bed to stand. Josephine reached out and seized Paul's arm, but he gently removed her hand.

Paul stepped off the bed and walked around it towards his father, who was dressed in a white T-shirt and blue jeans.

"Dad," Paul said gently.

"She thinks I'm some kinda heediot. Bout she's pregnant! I told you I don't want no pickney yet." Jacob screamed out the bedroom door to someone.

Whoever Paul's dad was talking to began to climb the stairs.

"You're a coward! You promised if I were to get pregnant, you'd stand by me."

Paul's jaw dropped in astonishment, his eyes transfixed upon the staircase.

"Mum," Paul muttered.

Paul's mother came to the top and stood in the doorway conversing with Jacob. She did not acknowledge Josephine upon the bed or her son standing directly behind his father.

You're so slim, Paul thought.

"Yeah! When I'm ready," Jacob replied.

"I went against my parents' wishes for you - you've just proven them right," Paul's mum said.

"You said you were on the pill?" Jacob responded.

"I was."

"Was or are? Two different tings! You uh tek me for some heediot!" Paul's dad raged, his Jamaican accent commandeering his tongue.

"I am on the pill, you ignorant fool; it doesn't always work."

Jacob began to laugh.

"You think this is funny; you'd better play your part; you know I don't believe in abortion," Paul's mum stated.

Jacob slammed the top of the wooden drawer, spun around, his teeth bared in a growl, and marched directly through Paul towards Paul's mother.

Paul attempted to seize his father, but his hands passed through his shoulders.

"Yo! Move from my mum!" Paul screamed at his dad.

Josephine raised her hands to cover her mouth.

Jacob went right up to Paul's mother's face until their noses were nearly touching.

"Your brudah ain't worth nothing, your mo-mah ain't worth nothing, your far-da and the whole uh dem ain't worth a penny. At least you'll have one family member with sumting uh gwan." Paul's father shouted.

Paul's mother stood silently observing her boyfriend, her facial expression conveying utter shock.

They remained like that for several seconds, neither moving nor uttering a word until she spoke.

"Get out." she whispered.

Jacob didn't budge. Paul's mother gritted her teeth, and her eyes became moist, raging-red-ovals.

"Get! The! Hell! Out!!!" She screamed.

Jacob sniggered.

"I was leaving anyway."

He turned from her, seized the bag he had filled, and then slipped past her, down the stairs and out the front door.

Paul's mother remained motionless for a moment, gazing at a spot on the floor, then she began to cry, sinking to her knees.

Paul's legs felt weak, and he knelt before his mother, attempting to embrace her, his hands passing through his mum at every attempt.

"Mumma - don't cry.. Mumma don't cry." Paul repeated through tears. Josephine hurried off the bed, sank to her knees behind Paul, and wrapped her arms around his waist.

Josephine buried her head between his shoulder blades and tenderly patted his stomach to console him. They both shut their eyes, and when they reopened them, they were in the dark.

They were situated on a torn piece of sponge, which had cushioned their fall through the roof of a small outhouse.

They remained in that embrace for a minute, weeping, until Paul stopped.

Josephine eventually released him, gradually rising and placing her hand upon his shoulder. Paul stood up as well.

They aided one another off the uneven surface of the sponge and down onto the floor.

Paul appeared dazed; Josephine recognised the expression of fresh anguish, for her body had once been the dwelling of sorrow so dark and profound that she was uncertain if she would ever witness the light again.

"Did that just happen? I mean, what on earth, man." Paul said.

"We don't have to talk about it," Josephine responded.

"I always thought my mother had pushed him away, and I believed her attitude was why I never had a father around," Paul said.

Josephine rested her hand upon his shoulder.

"You're better off without him; not every father makes for a good dad," Josephine replied.

Paul exhaled a deep breath.

"I need to get out of here," Paul stated.

Josephine was reluctant to agree; the prospect of being home alone until 6am with all the peculiar incidents transpiring was nothing less than terrifying.

"Yeah. About that. When we get back, will you stay with me till the morning?" Josephine asked.

"I was gonna ask you the same thing. I can't go home early anyway, or my mum'll know I lied, I'd never see outside again." Paul said.

The pair exited the outhouse and looked up to where they had fallen from.

Their eyes widened in astonishment as the wall they had toppled off was far higher than it had seemed earlier. They both pondered how fortunate they were to have survived.

They exchanged glances, then peered over their shoulders towards a building situated at the other end of the yard, some two hundred metres away.

The building was designed as a large white clown's head with two windows acting as eyes.
Colour-changing neon lights shone out the windows

from within the building, casting beams across the yard.

The clown's mouth was a smile curved around two massive doors painted as white teeth.

The yard contained small fairground rides scattered about. None of them were activated.

The tall walls encircling the yard were topped with large shards of broken glass.

"We can't go over the wall. Looks like we'll have to go through the building," Josephine said in a reluctant murmur.

"Is that building meant to be a clown's head or something?" Paul queried.

Josephine observed it.

"Yeah. Looks weird. I wonder what's inside?" Josephine said.

They both fell silent. Then Paul spoke up.

"Well. It is what it is. We have no choice. Come." Paul said.

The Heavens 1.1

"Oh dear, we have a problem; he-who-shall-not-be-named is interfering with them," Istustaya said.

"Yes, because you insisted we send Paul back and interfered first! You know it leaves things open for both sides now."

Istustaya regarded Hemsut.

"Can I be honest with you? It isn't the first time I've been involved."

Hemsut's eyes grew wide.

"What!" Hemsut said.

"There may have been a letter with instructions for somebody to help them," Istustaya declared.

Hemsut shook her head.

"Is it really? Surprise. Surprise." Hemsut said.

Istustaya opened the book (Deja vu) and presented it to Hemsut.

"They were stuck in a tight spot after you gave Paul another chance, so I sent a letter back and presented Jason with a few choices to see if he would help or not."

"Oh, Istustaya. You are getting too involved. It's getting messy," Hemsut stated.

"At least Jason's found his path; that's one for the Father," Istustaya responded.

"Listen. It's like I have to keep reminding you. Although we are free to utilise our gifts, it does not mean we are absolved from the repercussions of our decisions, you have to remember this. Anyway, let's check in on them." Hemsut said.

Hemsut formed a circle with her hands in the air, and within it, a shimmering vision appeared of Paul and Josephine approaching the clown house. Hemsut and Istustaya looked on.

Hemsut shook her head.

"This doesn't look good," Hemsut said of the sinister-looking building.

"You should leave this now; I think you could be making things worse," Hemsut added.

Istustaya looked away from the vision in thought.

"What is it about these two?" Hemsut asked, concerned.

"I don't know yet, but their pages are pure and clean. It's very rare one finds that in people. If these two proceed as I anticipate, they shall accomplish remarkable feats on Earth." Istustaya said.

"Well, they'll have to get through that building first, and you know the rules; Paul doesn't have any more goes left." Hemsut stated, referring to his lives.

"Well, let's hope they can," Istustaya responded, a glint in her eye.

Fun house

Josephine and Paul approached the eccentric-looking building. The doors swung open as they reached within fifty feet, and a lengthy red carpet, fashioned as a tongue, unrolled itself towards them. The pair stopped and observed the sight in astonishment.

A short, plump man emerged from the doorway and stood to the side of the entrance.

He was dressed as a combination of a clown and a ringmaster. He was not well-groomed.

His face was painted white with clown makeup applied. Stubble protruded through the paint.

His red ringmaster coat was exceedingly tight. His black boots were scuffed all over. His large belly strained the fit of the shirt, causing the buttons to be pushed out; the flesh from his stomach swelled in the gaps.

"Roll up! Roll up!" The Ringmaster shouted before he went into a coughing fit.

"Sorry about that, kids! Roll up! Roll up! Come play and stay for as long as you may!" The Ringmaster continued, scratching his backside aggressively.

Josephine displayed a look of revulsion at his repugnant behaviour. Paul gazed at Josephine and then down at the red carpet, at their feet.

"Come on in, guys. The games and sweets are free! You can stay as long as you like."

Josephine and Paul exchanged glances. Paul signalled for them to turn their backs to him in order to converse privately.

They both spoke in a whisper.

"I don't think so," Josephine stated.

"I know what you're saying. But we don't have any other options." Paul replied.

Josephine glanced over her shoulder at the Ringmaster, who was now scratching his armpits and placing his fingers to his nose to inhale the scent.

"Errr. He's scratching his nasty armpits," Josephine reported.

Paul looked over, then back.

"Who cares? I want to get out of here, and it's looking like the only way back out to the road is through there." Paul stated.

"I hear what you're saying, but given all the weird stuff going on, can we really trust it?" Josephine questioned.

"Look. The walls are too high. There are no other buildings to go through. Do you have any other ideas?" Paul reasoned.

Josephine closed her eyes to think.

"Hey, you guys! We're an attraction that needs traction, That's all," the Ringmaster shouted.

The pair looked back at him, then back to themselves.

"Why's the entrance at the back of the building and not the front?" Josephine questioned Paul.

Paul shrugged.

"This isn't our main entrance; it's our back entrance to our soon-to-be-in-operation funfair. The boss saw you on our security cameras and wanted me to call the police, but I convinced her to let you in so we could get more feedback on the business," the Ringmaster answered.

Paul looked at Josephine as if to say - *See. He's got all the right answers.*

"How did he hear that?" Josephine whispered to Paul.

"I got good hearing, darling. I eats me carrots and greens," the Ringmaster joked.

Paul shrugged.

Josephine and Paul turned to face him.

The Ringmaster performed a jig whilst waving jazz hands, shifting his weight from one side to the other.

"You get on the tongue, take a ride and see what's on the other side!" The Ringmaster rhymed.

Paul and Josephine exchanged glances for confirmation. Then they both nodded and stepped onto the tongue, which swiftly retracted, causing them to lose their balance. They fell to their knees and were dragged into the building, unable to stand.

As they were pulled past the Ringmaster, shrieking, his brow had furrowed, and his happy-go-lucky grin had transformed into a sinister smile.

Josephine and Paul were delivered into an arcade and gaming hall.

They quickly got up and ran back towards the door, but it had slammed shut and locked the moment they were inside.

The sound of the Ringmaster's cackling could be heard.

Josephine struck the door with her fist.

"Open this door now! Let us out!" She screamed as she battered the door.

Paul looked across the gaming hall.

The premises were decorated in black matt paint, with bright LEDs on both the floor and walls, carving out a path to traverse the building. Revolving LEDs flash and rotate from above, fading one colour into the next.

The delectable aroma of popcorn and candy floss hung heavy in the air.

The sounds of the arcade and various game machines vied for dominance.

The place was 'Trocadero' on steroids.

Paul gazed up at the large signage suspended in the middle of the hall. It read,

'All games are free upon entering our contract. You have entered into a contract with us as soon as you commence playing. All candyfloss and confectionery are free upon entering a contract. You have entered into a contract with us the moment you consume any candy floss or confectionery. All beverages are free. The moment you take a sip of a beverage, you have entered into a contract with us. Always read the terms and conditions before each game or at every stall or vendor. Enjoy yourselves!'

"Paul!"

Paul turned to regard Josephine.

"Ha."

"The door's locked. We can't get out." Josephine said.

Paul shrugged.

"Probably part of the experience. Some kind of act or whatever." Paul reasoned.

"No, it isn't; something isn't right," Josephine responds.

Paul gazed up at the signage once more.

"Are you even listening?" Josephine asked.

"We need to find a way out." Josephine continued.

"Hold on, nah. Let's have a little fun. The games and sweets are free," Paul said.

Josephine shook her head in dissent.

"Nothing in life is ever free. My father always said that."

"Well, it is here; it says so," Paul responded, pointing up at the signage.

Josephine read it.

"Yeah. But what's in the terms and conditions?" Josephine questioned.

"Look. All they probably want is our feedback, like the clown at the door said." Paul replied.

"Nah. Okay. Tell me this. Where are all the kids or workers?" Josephine queried.

Paul looked about in-between the machines. There were children scattered around playing games.

"Look, they're all playing," Paul responded.

"You're ignoring stuff because you want to play computer games," Josephine replied in a huff.

Paul pulled a face and shrugged.

"Yeah, I do like arcades. Nothing wrong with that. Look, just give me half an hour, and then we'll go." Paul stated.

Josephine fell silent.

"You can stay here if you want, and I'll be back in a minute," Paul suggested.

"You want us to split up?" Josephine asked.

"If you don't want to split, then come with me."
Paul pleaded.

"Okay. How about we talk to some of the kids and
see what this place is really about?" Josephine
suggested.

"Alright," Paul replied.

They walked away from the entrance and ventured
into the sea of arcade machines. The arcade machines
outnumbered the children by a ratio of ten to one.

They slowed to a stop at a boy playing 'Gran
Tourismo' His eyes were glazed. Heavy bags hung
beneath them. He looked young in body, but his face
appeared slightly older than his perceived age.

They stood on either side of the boy's racing chair,
observing him play.

He did not look as if he was enjoying it, tutting,
groaning, and mumbling under his breath. He had
been in the lead, swerved, and was pushed back into
third place, and lost.

He released the steering wheel and placed both
hands on top of his head in an obvious sign of stress.
He then closed his eyes and remained still. The game
waited to be started again.

Josephine and Paul exchanged glances.

Paul signalled that they should go.

They ventured further into the gaming hall, where
a candyfloss vendor stood beside a portable yellow
candyfloss machine on four large baby-blue wheels.

"I love candyfloss," Josephine said to Paul, leaving
his side and going to the vendor.

Paul watched her.

She returned empty-handed.

"Where is it?" Paul asked.

"I asked for the terms and conditions and he got funny with me."

"Terms and conditions. You a lawyer now, yeah?" Paul laughed.

"Does it not say at the entrance to read the terms and conditions?" Josephine questioned.

"Yeah, it's all part of the theatrics, innit," Paul responded.

A young woman approached and passed between them, her eyes glazed as if she had been awake for days.

"Candyfloss, my dear?" The candyfloss vendor enquired of the passing girl.

"I can't start that; I can't drink or eat anything. I just need to play until I win. I need to get home," the girl mumbled as she walked, her head held straight, taking fast-paced strides.

Josephine and Paul regarded one another, perplexed.

They progressed further into the gaming hall.

"I ain't gonna lie. You might be onto something still. This place feels a bit mad." Paul said.

"A bit mad. Something is seriously wrong with these kids and the workers."

"Hmmm," Paul responded.

"I think it's time to go," Josephine said.

"Maybe. Look. Give it twenty minutes." Paul proposed.

"Twenty minutes!" Josephine responded.

"Alright. Ten!"

Josephine gazed into the distance, contemplating.

"Fifteen, and that's it." She reasoned.

"Deal."

They encountered more youths playing arcade games, muttering and grumbling under their breath. The young people were so intent on winning that they seemed to have forgotten to enjoy themselves.

They reached a crossroads in the walkway, dividing the hall into four quarters.

To their right, about fifty metres away, a girl was engaged in a dancing game, whilst on their left, Paul spotted 'Street Fighter 2 Turbo'.

They both looked at their respective arcades and then at each other.

"Meet back here in a couple of minutes?" Josephine suggested.

"Read my mind," Paul said.

Josephine proceeded towards the dancing game, whilst Paul headed for 'Street Fighter'.

Paul approached and stood beside the boy, who was feverishly pummelling buttons and manoeuvring the joystick.

The boy was facing off against M. Bison, the final boss, who was normally moderately difficult, but this version of the game appeared to be insane. M. Bison was moving at speeds that Paul had never seen, and within seconds, the boy had been defeated.

"Game Over!" the arcade screamed.

The boy surrendered the controller, buried his head in his hands, and remained motionless.

After several seconds of the boy being hunched over, Paul stepped nearer and placed his hand on his back.

"Bro, you alright?" Paul asked.

The boy was slow to acknowledge him.

When he did respond, he seemed distressed.

"I just can't beat him, no matter how hard I try. Can you?" the boy asked Paul.

Paul looked at the screen. He loved 'Street Fighter 2'; it was one of his favourite games.

But this was 'Street Fighter 2 Turbo', which had just been released that summer, and cost an additional £1 to play at home.

Paul never had enough money to have a go, so the prospect of unlimited play was enticing.

"Go on. One go can't hurt," the boy said.

Paul regarded the boy, then the joystick and then the screen; the timer counted down from the previous game.

10!

9!

8!

7!

"One go should be cool, innit?" Paul said, looking for assurance from the boy.

The boy nodded and smiled.

"Go on," the boy said.

The boy's gaze shifted from Paul's face to Paul's hands.

Paul grabbed the joystick. His other hand hovered above the button to start the game.

This seemed to excite the boy somewhat.

From Paul's left, someone struck Paul's hand away from the button.

"Don't do it, bro!"

Paul stepped back from the machine.

"Raaah. What're you doing!" Paul shouted.

"They won't let you win. And if you play for him, you'll take his place here," the guy said.

Paul stared, amazed, at who was standing before him.

"Oh, my days, Isaac!" Paul said, stepping closer.

"You can never beat the game, bro!" Isaac said.

"What you on about?" Paul asked.

Isaac stepped closer, his eyes wide. He pointed at Paul.

"Read the small print on the screen before you play. Ask for the terms before you eat or drink." Isaac screamed.

Paul retreated from him. At the same time, two burly security guards approached and seized Isaac by his arms and legs.

Isaac began to sob and wail, trying his best to break free of them.

Josephine stood a few steps back from a girl feverishly tapping the lights flashing across the dance mat. The music is intense.

The girl playing is swift, but no person on Earth could match the pace of the machine.

Josephine looked at the girl's profile. The girl's eyes were wide. Her cheeks puffed in and out in an attempt to regulate her breathing. Her legs could not keep up with her intentions.

Josephine scrutinised her feet once more, and upon closer inspection, was astounded to discover that the girl's fervent dancing had destroyed the soles of her shoes; only the upper part of the trainers remained.

The arcade's 'Techno' music stopped, "Game Over! Want to try again?" the arcade sounded.

The girl turned around from the game, and Josephine was astonished, as the girl was not a girl at all; but a petite, fully grown woman.

"You want a turn? It's really fun. I've been playing for years," she said, cracking her neck.

"Others want the games to end, but not me. Dancing is soooo fun. Don't you think? Maybe we can dance together!" The woman suggested with a giggle.

Josephine took a step back. The woman watched Josephine; her gaze was steely, and behind her cheerful demeanour lay something far more menacing.

"Na, no, thanks," Josephine said before turning and heading back to get Paul; she looked over her shoulder, and the woman was ambling up to get back on the game.

Josephine encountered Paul as he was searching for her.

"Yeah. You see that fifteen minutes! Forget that! We need to leave now!" Paul said.

"Oh, now you agree," Josephine replied.

"Yeah, I just met someone I know,"

"Is it really?"

The pair commenced walking, surveying the building for an exit.

"Yeah. Two security guards just came out of nowhere and took him away."

"What? Why?"

"I was about to play, and he started telling me not to, then two security guards picked him up by his arms and legs and took him. They said he had breached the terms of his contract." Paul elaborated.

"Contract?" Josephine said.

They pass a young man preparing to use a punching arcade. His long-sleeved shirt is now sleeveless, and the torn-off sleeves are wrapped around his knuckles. Once set, he runs up and punches the ball so forcefully that it shakes the entire arcade, but the punch only registers a meagre five hundred points.

"That isn't even the mad part," Paul stated, staring at the boxer who began pacing in circles, tapping the sides of his head with the open palms of his hands.

"No," Josephine said.

"Nah. The maddest ting about it is that Isaac has been missing for the past three years. Have you heard this lyric? Shout out to Isaac who never came back; emcees from around our way spit it over music. Have you not heard it?" Paul asked Josephine.

"Can't say I have,"

"You must have at least seen the tags all over Harlesden. Isaac with a question mark after his name."

That she had seen. The graffiti was on the rear and sides of buses and on walls throughout their area.

"Yes, I have," Josephine said.

"Yeah, well that was him they just took. He's been here all along."

"Maybe this place is like a travelling circus or something? Maybe he's joined them," Josephine said, trying to understand it all.

"Nah, man. Isaac was a street yute. He weren't joining no frigging circus. I don't think he's here out of choice. I don't think any of them are." Paul said, looking around.

Josephine grew pensive.

"So what's keeping them here?" She questioned.

"I never had a chance to ask him," Paul said sarcastically.

"The contract. The terms and conditions." Josephine said.

"Yeah. Must be that." Paul responded.

"You see what I was saying. Well, that girl over there was in fact a woman dressed as a child. Her shoes never had soles; she looked like she'd been on that game forever!"

Paul shook his head.

"What the hell is going on in this place?" Paul questioned.

"I don't know, but we need to get out."

Paul took the lead, with Josephine following, their heads on swivel, surveying the sea of arcades, confectionery and drink stands.

It appeared that young people were everywhere, but upon closer inspection, some were in fact more mature. A few were barefoot, and their jumpers and T-shirts were worn like crop tops. These individuals were not adhering to some kind of fashion. They had simply been there for such a prolonged period that they had outgrown their clothes and footwear.

They played the games, drank and ate as if their very lives hinged upon it. On the surface, it looked like every child's dream: free games, drinks, and sweets, but upon real scrutiny, it didn't look fun at all; in fact, it looked like torture.

Paul and Josephine turned a corner and encountered a young lady seated on the floor, her legs spread. She was surrounded by an assortment of confectionery. Tufts of pink candyfloss were in her hands, sprouting from her pockets, and protruding from the corners of her mouth. Toffees were hanging off and stuck to her jumper. Her eyeballs were rolled back into her skull.

It appeared as if she had eaten herself into a sugar-induced comatose state.

They slowed down as they approached her, taking in the dreadful sight.

"Jesus," Paul murmured.

"Look. Exit." Josephine said, raising her voice.

A large exit sign was illuminated in the distance.

Their steady walk now became a jog, which then turned into a frantic run towards freedom.

They wove in and out of aisles and rows of deafening gaming machines until they reached an open area where the arcades and vending machines ended, revealing a neon-lit red floor that stretched fifty metres wide and long.

At the other end of it was the exit.

Between the exit and them stood an extremely tall woman wearing a long dress that covered her feet and touched the floor.

The hall fell into pin-drop silence as all the arcades switched off, and all the lighting was redirected to them.

"Leaving already?" The woman asked, looking between the pair.

Josephine and Paul looked at each other, then behind themselves. All those who had been playing the arcades had now assembled behind them.

Josephine nudged Paul in the side.

Paul regarded her, then the woman.

"Yeah, we have to get home. Our parents will be looking for us. We had fun, though."

The woman smiled warmly.

"Did you? You didn't eat, drink or play any of our games. That's such a shame," the woman said.

"Errr." Paul began.

"I was told a friend of yours said some very strange things to you earlier," the woman continued.

Josephine swallowed.

"Isaac." the woman said, clicking her fingers.

Isaac emerged from the crowd, circled Paul and Josephine, and positioned himself beside the woman.

She leant in and whispered into Isaac's ear.

He nodded.

"Listen, bro, I was acting a bit crazy earlier, got a bit carried away you know." Isaac announced.

The woman rested her hand upon Isaac's shoulder and gently massaged it.

"This place is zang bro. You can play, eat and drink as much as you desire. There are no rules, blud. No one's telling you what to do or when to do it; there's uh couple of nice gullies in 'ere as well, you get me. Soon, the fair outside will be completed, and we can go on the bumper cars and other rides too." Isaac said as if he were reading from a script.

The woman observed Paul, awaiting his response.

Paul looked at Josephine, then returned his gaze to Isaac.

"Nah bro, this place is buki; you said so," Paul responded, looking Isaac straight in the eye.

Isaac looked to the woman, and then downwards at the floor.

"I hope Isaac has reassured you. Will you stay for one game now?" the woman asked.

Paul paused to ponder. Then he replied.

"Okay. I'll play one game on one condition. If I win, everyone goes free with me." Paul said.

The challenge elicited murmurs from the crowd.

Josephine regarded Paul with disbelief.

"What're you doing?" Josephine asked, grabbing his forearm.

"It's cool," Paul responded.

"No. It. Isn't. Nobody can win here, you idiot." Josephine whispered to Paul.

"Ahhh. How noble. You do you know how it works here?" The woman asked.

"No," Paul replied.

"It's simple. If you play, eat or drink, you have entered into our contract by doing so. You must consume a full portion of food or drink to fulfil a contractual obligation. You must complete one of the games to fulfil your contractual obligation." The woman said.

"Yeah, but your portions are not humanly possible to eat or drink, and the games are ridiculously difficult. That's not fair." Josephine interjected.

"They should have read the terms and conditions. It is all there." The woman responded.

"So because we haven't played, drunk, or eaten anything, we can leave now if we want?" Paul asked.

The woman bowed her head and stated 'correct', then waved her hand through the air, and the exit door's glass became transparent, unveiling the bustle of Soho outside. The door's locks disengaged.

Josephine and Paul's eyes widened at the magical feat.

Paul spun around, thinking everyone would be streaming towards the exit, but instead, they retreated further back, bunched up like wildebeest in the presence of a lion.

They were petrified.

Paul looked at the woman in disbelief. She appeared smug.

"You're wondering why they don't leave. They can't. I have a lien on their souls. Everything comes at a cost, even enjoyment. When they fulfil their contract, they get it back," the woman said.

Josephine tapped Paul's leg.

"Let's go while we still have a chance,"Josephine whispered.

'We can't leave these people here,' Paul whispered back.

Josephine fell silent.

"Just trust me," Paul said.

She shook her head from side to side to say 'no'.

"I hope you know what you're doing," Josephine responded.

"You go, and I'll meet you outside," Paul insisted.

Josephine looked at the exit, then at the woman, and then back at Paul.

"No. We stay together."

"I need a decision. If you wish to leave, do so now. If not, choose your game and let us proceed with it," the woman said.

"I'll take the boxing game. What do I have to do to clock it?"

Josephine's mouth fell open, her eyes wide.

"Boxing game!" Josephine pronounced.

Paul did not respond.

The woman tilted her head to one side, intrigued with Paul's choice.

"A score of 999." The woman said.

"For everyone's freedom, yeah."

The woman scrutinised Paul as if she were having second thoughts.

"As agreed." The woman eventually responded.

"Do I have your word?" Paul asked.

The woman laughed and nodded.

"My name is Atë, and my word is my bond; I am the owner and rule maker here. In three turns, if you can achieve a score of 999 on the punch machine, all shall be liberated, with their souls."

"Deal," Paul said.

Josephine began to feel nauseous. She turned and faced Paul, drawing close, her back to the woman.

"Paul, what are you doing? You're going to get trapped here. We have a chance to leave; we should take it. They made their choice," Josephine said.

"I've got this," Paul reassured.

"No, you haven't. That guy punching the machine was way bigger than you, and look how low his score was."

"Truss me, I hold the record for that machine in North West," Paul said.

Josephine sighed, defeated.

"Come now. Let the game begin," Atë said as she walked past Paul, dividing the crowd. Paul followed the woman, with Josephine following him and the entire group of trapped gamers following her.

Josephine glanced over her shoulder at the horde behind. They appeared soulless.

They were grey in complexion. Death hovered about them like autumn mist over an English moor. *Paul shall join them if he fails here, she* pondered. *His friends and family will likely blame me for his disappearance.* The prospect sent a shiver through her.

They approached and stopped at the boxing game.

Atë stepped beside the inactive arcade and touched its side. Energy coursed through it, and it sprang to life, one LED after the next.

Paul took a deep breath.

Josephine stood just behind him.

Paul turned and looked at her; her eyes were shiny, as though she were on the verge of tears.

"Press the button at the top to commence," Atë requested.

Paul looked away from Josephine and faced the machine.

He reached up and pressed the button. The boxing ball was unlocked and lowered, ready to be struck.

Paul cracked his neck and knuckles. He paused momentarily, then leant back and swung at the ball, striking it with all his might. It barely moved. The score registered at 300.

Josephine closed her eyes.

"One attempt down. Two to go," Atë said.

Paul exhaled.

The ball reset.

Paul closed his eyes to concentrate and block out all distractions.

He approached the side of the ball, leaned back, paused briefly, and then swung.

The impact did not translate to the ball's movement, and his score was even lower than before. The ball's arm was clearly tightened, hindering smooth movement.

Even Mike Tyson would have struggled to achieve a high score on the game.

The crowd began to murmur, and some even departed, retreating into the darkness of the gaming hall, resigning themselves to his defeat.

"This is your last chance." Josephine said, her voice raised.

"You better have a plan." Josephine continued.

"That was your second attempt. This will be your final go," Atë stated.

Paul offered Atë the warmest smile he could muster.

Josephine looked at him as if he were deranged.

Paul stepped onto the opposite side of the ball and positioned himself.

He drew his fist back over his shoulder and delivered a straight right, glancing the ball and following through past it, striking the rear of the arcade. Josephine gasped and Atë grinned. Paul stood upright and watched the screen.

The numbers began to run.

200

300

400

500

Atë's smile became a frown.

600

Josephine's jaw dropped.

700

800

999

Atë recoiled from the machine like a cockroach exposed to a sudden glare of light.

"How?!!" Atë shouted.

The crowd erupted, screaming and hollering.

"Hooow!!!" Atë snarled, stepping further back into the shadows, her black dress curling around her in a cocoon-like spiral.

The place started to shake as if in the grip of an earthquake. The arcades began to topple this way and that, falling all over the place.

Atë's workers began to retreat into the shadows, following Atë - shedding their human guises, their true bodily forms revealed: gargoyle-like creatures. Wings sprang from their backs, and they flapped upwards towards the ceiling now open to the night sky.

The exit doors sprang open.

"Everyone get to the exit!" Someone shouted.

The crowd began to move, all sprinting at full pace. Colour returned to their flesh.

People leapt through the open doors and tumbled out onto Soho's street. Josephine and Paul were the last to leave. When they looked back, the building was a Chinese restaurant with diners who had stopped eating and were now baffled, wondering where Josephine and Paul had appeared from.

*****

"Atë!" Istustaya said, surprised.

"Isn't that Zeus's daughter?" Hemsut replied.

"Fallen. Daughter." Istustaya added.

"What's she doing here? This isn't even her reality," Istustaya continued.

"I don't know, but something strange is happening."

Istustaya went to her book 'Deja vu'.

"Says here time travel or dimension jumping can cause rips and tears in the walls of time and reality."

"That must be it."

"But who is travelling through time?" Hamsut queried.

"I don't know, my eye only has jurisdiction over this realm. Anyway, we'll soon find out. In the meantime, and most importantly, we must inform Father so he can contact Olympus. Zeus has to do something about this."

"Yes, tell him he has a responsibility to come and collect his daughter."

*****

Josephine and Paul looked around the street. They had anticipated fifty to a hundred other youths, teens and adults from the gaming hall, but it was only them and the natural flow of West End human traffic.

They turned in circles, searching for the rest.

"Where are they?" Josephine questioned.

Paul looked concerned.

"I don't know. I made it clear that everyone should be free. That was the deal."

"Well, it's just us," Josephine said.

"Nah, that ain't right. We had an agreement." Paul responded.

Josephine shrugged.

"What can we do about it now?"

Paul was far from fond of Josephine's flippant response.

After five minutes of deliberation, they began making their way towards Oxford St.

The notion of attending the party had long since passed; they were weary, scared and craved the comfort of familiar surroundings.

"I cannot believe that just happened. How did you do it?" Josephine asked.

"Well. My uncle Juicy used to box."

"Oh, he taught you how to punch?" Josephine interjected.

"Yeah, he did, but that's not the point. Anyway, he got beaten on the boxing machine at Roundwood funfair by a smaller guy a couple of years ago. My uncle kept pushing coins into the machine to beat his score, but he couldn't do it no matter how hard he tried. Anyway, after spending almost an hour there, he got speaking with a guy who works at the fair who told him that those machines had light sensors that registered how fast objects went past them. He said the guy simply punched the ball but carried on past it to register a high score. I never forgot what that man said, it stuck in my mind. That's how I knew I could beat it." Paul explained.

"Oh my goodness. That's so amazing."

"Yeah, all for nothing now, though. They didn't get out." Paul said.

"Well, there's nothing we can do about that. At least we're good."

Paul slowed his pace.

"Wow, don't you ever think of anyone but yourself?" Paul asked.

Josephine stopped, and so did Paul.

"What?"

"You heard me. You're being mad, selfish man." Paul continued.

"So because I didn't want us to be trapped in some endless arcade hall I'm selfish?"

"I hear that, but-"

"You might not want to see your mum or brother again, but I do. I didn't leave my home not to return for the sake of strangers." Josephine replied.

Paul pondered her perspective. She had a valid point.

"Look. I don't want to argue. I just want to go home now. I'm frightened, I don't understand what's going on, and my mind is tired. Do you still have that money for a cab?" Josephine asked.

Paul began patting his pockets.

"Don't tell me you've lost it," Josephine said, looking out towards the road at taxis whizzing up and down - their roof lights illuminated yellow.

Paul continued to search himself. He started shaking his head.

"Think it's gone," Paul said.

"Damn!"

"Yeah, definitely gone. We'll have to bump it." Paul confirmed, waving above his head to summon a taxi.

"Bump a cab? As in, not pay? Me?" Josephine said, her hands touching her breastbone.

"Look, what other options do we have?" Paul said.

A taxi slowed to a halt alongside them.

"Well, who hasn't got morals now, eh? That's theft, I don't do things like that; I'd rather walk." Josephine protested.

Paul looked back at her, and she looked at him. Paul sniggered to himself.

"You know what! I should never have invited you..."

Josephine's mouth opened and froze - stuck in an O.

"What?" She uttered.

"You heard me! All of this is because I was trying to do the right thing. Now, look at the madness we're in. None of this would have happened if I had got in the car with them lot." Paul responded.

Paul stared at her for a few seconds, then turned and peered into the taxi to speak to the driver.

"Where to?" The taxi man asked.

"Church Rd, Willesden," Paul replied.

Paul glanced back at Josephine.

"You coming or not?" Paul asked.

Josephine remained silent. She looked off as if he hadn't said a word.

"Fine by me!" Paul said.

With that, Paul opened the rear passenger door and slid inside.

The taxi driver pulled off and continued for a few seconds before pulling over again. He turned in his seat to face Paul.

"On second thoughts. That'll be ten pounds up front, mate," the taxi driver asked.

Paul cleared his throat.

"Ten pounds? Bu..But I thought I paid at the end?"

"Normally, but not you though. I need some insurance. I've dealt with your kind before. Running off without paying and all that, I don't have the time, the pace or the knees to be chasing passengers," the taxi man said.

Paul patted his pockets as if searching for the requested sum. He eventually abandoned the act.

"I must have lost it," Paul mumbled.

"Yeah, and I'm Prince of Persia. Get out, please," the taxi man responded.

With that, Paul opened the door and once more stepped out into the splendours of the West End.

Josephine strolled back towards Oxford Street, surrounded yet alone. Her mind was frantically jumping between what she had witnessed in the gaming hall, time travel, and Paul's ugly words, lurching around the chambers of her mind, going round and around on repeat.

I should never have invited you. I should never have invited you. I should never have invited you.

Josephine was tired now—tired of the day, tired of her life, tired of her brother being her brother, tired of feeling disconnected from everyone in the world, especially after the one person beyond her mother with whom she thought she had found something genuine had proved her wrong. She yearned for sleep, a lengthy, long night of slumber.

*****

Paul had walked back down towards Regent St - Josephine, nowhere to be seen.

Exhausted, he decided to sit on the steps of the 'Eros' statue. The Eros statue was a sculpture of a winged man poised on one foot, with a bow and arrow above a water fountain with numerous steps encircling the monument 360 degrees, allowing people to sit and stand beneath the statue.

Paul observed the advertisement screens of Piccadilly once again.

10pm felt like an eternity from when he was scheduled to return home the following day.

He could not simply arrive early; as his mother would not accept any reason he could muster and would not stop calling Fabian's home until she spoke to Fabian's mother, resulting in her uncovering the deception in which he had partaken.

He would never be allowed out again; in fact, none of them would, because Paul's mother would also make it her mission to ensure everybody else's parents knew about this; needless to say, the boys wouldn't be happy with him.

Paul's thoughts revisited his father and mother's interaction in the vision, then shifted to the gaming hall.

"I must be losing my mind. They must have been actors. Places like that don't exist, bro; time travel don't exist. None of this makes sense," Paul whispered to himself.

Josephine stood at the 98 bus stop, her finger searching the timetable and looking for the next bus heading home. *Half an hour,* she thought.

She opened her purse but could not see how much she had, owing to the unrelenting tears streaming down her face, blurring her vision.

She wiped her cheeks and eyes with her arm and emptied all the change out into her palm to get a better look. In addition to the money, the golden travel card also fell out. She passed the card through her fingers, analysing it.

*****

Paul's mind evoked Josephine. *She must be on her way home now, he thought. You should never have said those things. I can't even blame her if she never speaks to me again.* Paul took a deep breath and released it.

I can smooth it over; maybe you can, but first, you gotta get through tonight. You know what? I'll stay right here till morning; nothing ain't happening with all these people about.

With that, Paul looked out across the swarm of humans, moving in all directions, except for one—a man stood in the middle of the crowd, forcing everyone to circumnavigate him. He then began walking in Paul's direction.

The man's approach felt personal. He took large, pronounced strides and locked eyes with Paul.

A sense of unease swelled around Paul, and he shot up and began stumbling among and around people in an attempt to descend the monument and run; after seconds and a few choice words from people he had trodden on, Paul was down and running up Regents St towards Oxford Circus.

He glanced over his shoulder in the direction he had come and expected to see the man at his heels, but he was not there.

Paul shifted from an all-out run to a backwards jog, ready to pivot and sprint at the first sign of his pursuer.

As Paul passed a narrow side street, the man reached out, seized him, and yanked him into the narrow walkway before Paul had the chance to react.

Paul attempted to cry out, but the man had his hand over Paul's mouth, muffling his call.

The man then positioned his hands around Paul's throat, securing him in a chokehold.

"Stop moving!" The man hissed.

"Don't fight, I'm not trying to hurt you," the man stated.

"Get off me! Help! Help! Heeeelp!" Paul screamed, staring at the opening to the main road.

People were so absorbed in their own affairs that they did not even look.

"You're wasting precious time." The man said.

Paul ceased moving, realising the man was not applying any real pressure.

"Look, I'm going to let go. Run if you want, but please trust me. You need to hear me out."

The man released Paul and raised his hands above his head to demonstrate his peaceful intent. Paul looked at him from head to toe, then focused on his face. Paul recoiled in astonishment.

"Yo..Yo.. You look like -" Paul began.

"Me." Future Paul said to Paul through a parade of skinned teeth.

"Ha?" Paul said.

Future Paul nodded, lowering his arms to his sides.

"We're running out of time; you need to get to Josephine before she gets on that bus. You need to smooth things over. If she never speaks to you again and finds someone else, you. Sorry. I mean, we could end up with Beatrice." Future Paul stated.

"Wow, wow! Woooow! Are you telling me you're me from the future?" Paul asked.

"Yep, cannot believe it worked," Future Paul replied chuffed with himself.

"Rah! I'm proper gone, you know. Man's uh complete mad man now." Paul spoke to himself, walking in circles, both palms flat against his cheeks.

"Nope," Future Paul replied.

"Listen -" Future Paul said, pulling out a smartphone and looking at the screen.

Paul stepped back from him upon sight of the futuristic-looking device.

"What's that?" Paul asked about the smartphone.

"Don't worry about it. Our primary concern at present is reaching Josephine in time; or it's possible we get closer to getting with Beatrice." Future Paul said with a shiver.

Paul appeared perplexed.

"What? Who's Beatrice? And what's so bad about her?" Paul questioned.

"Everything! Trust me, I'm married to her now. She's uh power-mad psychopath! I've dedicated all my resources and time over the past five years to time travel in order to return and rectify this night."

"Whaaat! You mean to tell me you only time travelled to change your wife. Not to give me the lottery numbers, or..Or..Uh, tip on a horse or something - That's nuts!" Paul said.

"What do you think this is, Back to the Future? Besides, money isn't an issue, but the issue." Future Paul began.

"Wait! Sa-what you saying? We're rich?" Paul asked, his eyes sparkling.

Future Paul inhaled and exhaled a deep breath.

"Unfortunately..."

"Yeeeeeeeeeeees!" Paul shouted, jumping up and down on the spot.

"Oh. Hold on, wait. You said, unfortunately?" Paul stated, slowing to a stop.

"Look. We become wealthy through unethical means with Beatrice." Future Paul clarified.

"Unethical? How? Okay. Wait; if I go and meet Josephine now, that means I don't meet Beatrice, and I don't get dough?" Paul questioned.

Future Paul remained silent.

"Ha? Is that it or not?" Paul questioned.

"Man. I can't believe I was so annoying, can we walk and talk?" Future Paul said, shaking his head.

✳ ✳ ✳ ✳ ✳

Josephine stood out from the bus stop, people-watching. A man strolled past and stopped beside her, clutching a bundle of roses. She looked beyond his smile at his teeth for anything untoward, and at his back for wings like the gargoyles from the arcade hall—*human* she concluded.

The man extracted a single rose from the bunch and offered it for her to accept.

"A rose for a rose," remarked the man.

Josephine smiled.

"For me?" Josephine asked.

The man nodded.

"There it is; you're too young to look so old. Take." The man insisted.

Josephine accepted the gift.

"Have faith; the world feels better that way," the man said as he curtseyed, turned, and walked into the stream of people.

"You ought to be careful - taking things from strangers," a woman at the opposite end of the bus stop said. Josephine turned to face the woman. She was of mixed heritage, slender, with freckles and brownish hair. She was impeccably dressed and appeared remarkably familiar.

"Ha?" Josephine responded.

The woman regarded her in a peculiar manner, her eyelids partially narrowed, her lips pursed. Then she smiled and closed the distance between them.

Josephine stepped back, examining her hands and teeth, searching for signs of strange.

"Darling, I don't bite, but I have something you might want to hear."

$$* * * * *$$

Paul deliberately walked slowly to allow himself time to determine whether he wished to prevent himself from becoming exceedingly wealthy and meeting Beatrice (who sounded remarkably fit).

"Litsen, I don't think things will work out for me and Josephine anyway, we're too different. I mean, you know.." Paul said.

Future Paul laughed out loud.

"Errr, no I don't know, and neither do you. You're only fifteen," Future Paul teased.

Paul halted in his tracks, and people behind him muttered as they had to go around him.

"Mate, you came back to get me, not the other way round, yeah." Paul said.

Future Paul didn't respond. Instead, he glanced down at his smartphone.

"That one of them things from Qunatim leap?" Paul asked.

"Four minutes' walk. Five to spare. Come on, P, we've got to get moving." Future Paul said.

"I'm not going anywhere till you tell me what that is and why you keep staring at it," Paul demanded.

Future Paul showed him the smartphone interface. Google Maps on the screen.

"It's a smartphone, and I'm looking at Google Maps to see how much more time we have until Josephine's bus arrives versus our ETA," Future Paul said.

"Google? Smartphone? ETA?" Paul said.

"Google's like the Yellow Pages inside here. Smartphones are pretty cool. They have games, films and digital tools to help organise your life - applications for socialising, radio and more. ETA - estimated time of arrival. Now, can we keep going?" Future Paul explained and asked.

"Wow! So, you mean to tell me, there's a map telling you where to go, and a TV, radio and games, in that? That's Zang!" Paul said.

"Yep, they're called smartphones for a reason, but trust me, as they get smarter, we get dimmer. Oh yeah, youths don't say 'zang' anymore?" Future Paul said.

"Really, what do they say in…"

"2024. Calm, cold…" Future Paul responded.

"Calm blud..Hmmm." Paul said, rubbing his chin.

They continued on towards Oxford St.

"Do we ever get another Biggie?" Paul asked.

"Well, we do get this guy who sort of sounds like him - Gorilla Black or something like that, same voice but not even close lyrically."

Paul nodded.

"Tell me Nas is still alive in 2024?" Paul questioned.

"Yeah, but the last couple of albums have been iffy.." Future Paul said.

"No way," Paul responded.

Future Paul shrugged.

"Oh. Wait till you hear Kanye West. He's serious."

"kan-ye West. Hmm, okay. Black Pri-minister?" Paul asked.

Future Paul smiled.

"Not yet, but we do get a Black US President. And he gets two terms." Future Paul said.

Paul's mouth fell open.

"What! When?" Paul asked.

"No dates." Future Paul said.

"What's his name?" Paul asked.

"Can't say, might mess something up somewhere. Let's keep things general when discussing people who can affect the trajectory of the world."

"Wow! A Black President. That seems kinda impossible. Are you being for real?" Paul asked.

Future Paul shook his head from side to side.

"Nothing is impossible. If you believe it, you can achieve it. I'm here, aren't I?" Future Paul said.

Paul nodded to his future self.

"How could I forget. We do get a Prime Minister of colour. He's of Indian origin." Future Paul added.

"What! Yo! The future seems calm." Paul said with a wink.

Future Paul smiled.

They reached a hundred metres from the turn to get onto Oxford St

"Do computer graphics get any better than the SNES?"

"Oh yes!"

"No way! They cannot get better than StarFox or Donkey Kong."

"Wait till you play the PlayStation, one, two, three, four and five." Future Paul said.

"Play-station?" Paul repeated.

"Yep, Sony's console. Changes gaming forever." Future Paul explained.

"Sony makes computer games?" Paul asked.

"Yeah, and some pretty impressive high-definition flat-screen TVs. So clear it's like looking out a window."

Paul looked away in contemplation, his smile slowly fading.

"When does Mum die?" Paul mumbled.

Future Paul regarded him with a broad, beaming smile.

"Don't know, she's still alive in 2024. And still being a pain in our arse." Future Paul responded.

Paul's face lit up.

"Yes!" Paul shouted.

As they round the corner and the bus stop comes into view, Future Paul's face becomes thoughtful, his gaze fixed upon the small crowd waiting there.

They stopped walking some fifty metres from the bus stop.

"We have five minutes until her bus gets here. Look, there are two things I need to tell you," Future Paul said, looking at his phone's screen.

"In 2001, you, Jay, and Sam are sitting in Jay's bedroom; his dad comes in and offers you advice. Take it." Future Paul suggested.

Paul looked confused.

"Sam and Jay from school?" Paul asked.

"Yeah."

"But I hardly even speak to them."

"Well, they become good friends of ours. If you listen to Jay's dad, we can make a lot of money instead of making money with Beatrice. See, I'm still ensuring we get the bag," Future Paul said, patting Paul's shoulder.

"The bag? Okay. What's the advice?" Paul asked.

"It doesn't matter, just do it." Future Paul insisted.

"Okay. You still haven't told me what's up with Beatrice?" Paul asked.

"That's number two. She's pretty, absolutely gorgeous, and bad news for us. Do not, under any circumstances, get with anyone named Beatrice—and I mean under any circumstances. I cannot say any more than that." Future Paul said.

*****

"Paul will try to get you to be with him. Don't you dare. You've already seen how quickly he can switch, and it doesn't get any better in the future." The woman said as she walked Josephine down Oxford St, headed towards Bond St.

"How do you know all of this?" Josephine asked.

"I'm sort of a clairvoyant. You'd be wise to listen to me," the woman said, her eyes glued to Josephine's face.

"I don't need to be told; trust me, I'll never talk to him again after the things he said to me," Josephine replied.

The woman grinned.

"Good girl."

"Look, I have more to tell you about a man who may come to talk to you. Plus something very serious about Paul," the woman added, her eyes glistening.

*****

"Nooo! She isn't here!" Future Paul said, running around the bus stop, looking in all directions.

Paul observed Future Paul, as did everyone else. He appeared unhinged.

"Who you looking for, mate?" A man asked, having observed Future Paul's frantic behaviour.

"Young dark-skinned girl. She was just here," Future Paul said.

"Right. Seen her five minutes ago, she went that way with a woman," the man said.

"Yeah, a light-skinned Black lady, a bit shorter than you," a woman added.

Future Paul froze in place, gazing into the distance.

"You okay?" Paul asked.

Future Paul shook his head and chuckled.

"Beatrice.." Future Paul mumbled.

"What?" Paul said.

"Beatrice must be here; we've got to go now!" Future Paul said, turning on his heels and pulling Paul by the shoulder to move.

"I had a feeling she was on to me," Future Paul announced.

As they jogged towards Bond St, Future Paul began waving down taxis; one pulled up beside them outside McDonald's and rolled down the window.

"Where to, mate?" the taxi driver asked.

"Willesden!" Future Paul shouted, in between fighting for breath.

The taxi driver nodded.

Future Paul flung open the taxi door and forcefully pushed Paul inside. The taxi driver glanced over his shoulder and frowned at Future Paul's aggressive behaviour.

Future Paul caught him staring.

"My son, he's my son. We're running late," Future Paul said, making an excuse.

He closed the car door, and the taxi driver pulled away.

"You look on that side of the road, and I'll watch this side," Future Paul instructed Paul.

$$*****$$

Josephine and Beatrice approached Marble Arch, walking and scanning for an available black cab.

"Thanks for this," Josephine said.

"Don't mention it; I'm going the same way anyway. I'll get you home," Beatrice replied with a smile.

"You know, I've always been sceptical about palm readers and all those sorts of people. Mum got someone to communicate with my dad on the other side, and my brother and I never believed it, but nothing is impossible after tonight." Josephine said.

"Hmm," Beatrice responded.

Josephine looked at her; she seemed disinterested.

"You know, I never asked you your name?" Josephine said.

Beatrice smiled.

"Beatrice," Beatrice said, waving her hand above her head at a cab. The cab signalled and pulled over.

"Beatrice," Josephine repeated.

"That's my name; don't wear it out," Beatrice joked as she opened the cab door for Josephine to get in. Josephine slid in, and Beatrice followed suit.

"Where to, ladies?" the cabman asked.

Beatrice looked to Josephine, and Josephine met her gaze.

"Church Rd, Willesden, please?" Beatrice said.

Josephine's brow furrowed.

"Oh, you live on the estate as well?"

"Kind of," Beatrice smiled.

*****

Future Paul observed the mob of pedestrians on the street beside them.

"Are you looking?" Future Paul asked Paul sat behind him.

"For?" the taxi driver responded.

"Not you mate, him." Future Paul said, pointing behind him with his thumb.

"Oh." the taxi driver responded.

"Yeah, I am!" Paul replied.

"Can you slow it down a bit?" Future Paul asked the taxi driver.

"Your time, your money." The taxi driver responded as he slowed the taxi down.

They drove around the Marble Arch.

"Where do you think they would be headed?" Future Paul asked Paul.

"Back to the manor for sure," Paul said.

"Okay. Go down the Edgware Rd, please." Future Paul instructed the taxi driver.

Future Paul pulled out his smartphone and began looking at the Jubilee line tube map, considering that they may have jumped on the Tube at Bond St.

The light from the phone's screen illuminated Future Paul's face and the ceiling above. The taxi driver persistently glanced at Future Paul's hands using the mobile on his lap. Future Paul tried to conceal it as best he could.

They pulled up at a set of traffic lights. The taxi driver was so captivated by the phone that he had failed to notice the traffic lights changing from red to green. A cacophony of car horns erupted behind him.

"What's that then?" The taxi driver eventually inquired about the smartphone.

"Hey, eyes on the road, mate," Future Paul instructed.

Paul began to chuckle at the taxi driver's facial expression as he pulled away, glancing between the road ahead and the phone.

Future Paul put the phone away.

"What station would they get off at if they jumped on the Tube?" Future Paul asked Paul.

Paul paused momentarily to think.

"I don't know," Paul replied.

"Oh yeah, in those days, it was all about buses innit," Future Paul reminisced.

The taxi driver glanced at Future Paul when he said 'in those days'.

"Why?" Paul questioned.

"I know Beatrice; she's smart. She would've jumped on some form of transport to get out of the area quickly." Future Paul reasoned.

Paul nodded.

"Take us to Neasden Tube station, mate. Step on it!" Future Paul instructed the taxi driver.

The taxi driver did not respond, as he was preoccupied with observing the road and Future Paul's pocket where the smartphone was.

"Here, that thing you 'ad in your 'ands, that one of them Game Boys or something?" The taxi driver asked, leaving Edgware Road and turning left towards Warwick Avenue and the Harrow Road.

"Mate, you should have gone straight. Don't worry about the device; just speed up," Future Paul insisted.

"Device…Device, is that what it's called?" The taxi driver asked.

Paul laughed, observing the exchange between his future self and the taxi driver was amusing.

"Here, I'd love to go on your device, mate; how about this, the ride's free if you give me five minutes with it at the end of the trip. You don't understand how much I love computer games and all that," the taxi driver stated.

"If you speed up, I'll give you ten; how about that?" Future Paul responded.

The taxi driver's eyes gleamed, his foot pressed down, and his voice rose.

"First, I had a Commodore 64, then an Amiga, then I got the Master System 1 and 2, then a Mega Drive, which is still one of the best gaming systems ever. See, I'm loyal; you won't find a Nintendo around my 'ouse, nope! Currently saving for one of them, PlayStations. My wife thinks I'm a big kid, but look, every man needs something, right? Your vice could be drink, drugs, or even women. My vice is games and tech; I love 'em ta bits. That device looks out of this world! I bet it's from Japan; you know they're ten years ahead of us in technology, right? Them and the Germans. Ten minutes, yeah? You couldn't stretch it to fifteen, could you? I'd absolutely love it if you could?"

Future Paul tilted his head back and released a loud sigh. Paul burst out laughing.

They were delayed in traffic just past Royal Oak Tube station and were nearing a petrol station on their left at the tip of Harrow Road. Paul was familiar with this area as he attended school nearby.

The taxi driver wouldn't stop talking and somehow convinced Future Paul to allow him an hour with the smartphone. At that point, Future Paul would have agreed to any request to silence him.

"You think I'm just a taxi driver, don't you?" the taxi driver asked Future Paul.

"Yeah, but I bet you're gonna tell me different," Future Paul replied sarcastically.

The taxi driver chuckled and shook his head.

"Alright, son, no need to get sarky. Listen, mate, this just pays the bills. I've just applied for an internship with Apple Macintosh UK. You know 'em?" The taxi driver questioned.

"Yeah, I do." Future Paul responded.

"My wife thinks I'm bonkers, but I love technology - I think Apple Macintosh and Steve Jobs are on the verge of something big."

"Yeah, reckon? I wonder what that could be." Future Paul said with a smile.

Paul broke away from their discussion and scanned from left to right and behind them; he looked across the petrol station forecourt ahead.

A taxi driver was standing at a pump, refuelling his vehicle. Two people were moving about in the back seat of his taxi. Paul scrutinised further and first recognised Joesphine's cream cardigan. Then Josephine turned and gazed out of the rear window directly at Paul.

"Aye! I found them," Paul shouted.

Future Paul swivelled around.

Paul gestured out of the window at the taxi in the forecourt.

"Let's go!" Future Paul shouted, undoing his seat belt.

Paul attempted to open his door, but it wouldn't budge.

Josephine and Beatrice jumped out of their taxi and began running.

Future Paul faced the taxi driver.

"Open the bloody doors!" Future Paul shouted.

The taxi driver grinned and extended his open palm, wiggling his fingers. Future Paul glanced down at the outstretched hand, released a heavy sigh, reached into his pocket, and surrendered his iPhone to the taxi driver.

The taxi driver pressed a button, and the door locks released.

"You get on; I'll meet you further down the road—I promise," the taxi driver assured.

Mindful of the disruption to the space-time continuum and destiny, Paul was reluctant to leave the iPhone, but reasoned the screen was locked, so the taxi driver would be unable to access the technology within.

With that, both Pauls took off after Beatrice and Josephine, who had crossed the road and were heading down Sutherland Road (A side street), which coincidentally was where Paul's secondary school was.

The future Paul led the chase, shouting in pursuit.

"Beatrice! Stop this now!" Future Paul screamed.

Beatrice didn't look back—both she and Josephine were running blindly, taking random turns.

"Beatrice, you cannot stop this!" Future Paul shouted as Josephine began to slow with Beatrice virtually dragging her by the arm till her legs quit, too.

Beatrice and Josephine entered Edbrooke Road Playground, wheezing and fighting for breath.

The Pauls followed in pursuit.

Josephine and Beatrice stood in the centre of the playground with nowhere to go. Beatrice held Josephine by the arm.

"How on earth did you get here?" Future Paul asked Beatrice.

"That's irrelevant. You came back to help yourself hide Josephine's body better so you don't get caught in the future. I've told her all about you," Beatrice said, staring between both Paul and Josephine.

"What!!!" Both Pauls shouted in unison.

"Yeah, is that what tonight was all about? You planning to kill me?" Josephine shouted.

"Are you crazy?!" Paul responded.

Future Paul chuckled, shaking his head.

"You've told some lies in your time, Beatrice, but this takes the bloody biscuit. Tell her the truth and let us return to the future, or we may end up trapped here forever. Do you know that?" Future Paul asked Beatrice.

Beatrice regarded her husband, he pressing her buttons as he always knew how.

"That's a lie. You have a way back; you always plan ahead," Beatrice said.

"Yes! But I didn't plan for you to follow me here, and now that's probably caused some kind of rift in time and an issue with our return," Future Paul replied.

"Josephine! Why would you believe that? All I've done tonight is try to keep us safe," Paul said, staring at Josephine.

"Don't listen to him; he's a liar. Paul, if you get together with Josephine, you end up taking her life. It's an accident, but it happens, and you cover it up. The issue is her remains are uncovered in our time, and you go to jail. He's here to ensure you cover things up properly." Beatrice protested.

Josephine seemed distressed.

"Shut up, Beatrice! Tell them the damn truth about who you are and the despicable things you do to communities in the UK and abroad in the name of politics and money, dragging my good name down into the dirt. That is the real reason you're here, to try and hang on to power." Future Paul stated.

"I'm a politician; I do what I must. Challenging circumstances demand resolute choices. You, on the other hand, are a killer. I shall not allow you to commit the deed and hide the evidence from the law." Beatrice said, still gripping Josephine's arm.

Paul was astonished.

Future Paul shook his head.

"I have researched this. We have a time limit here, woman; if we remain beyond twenty-four hours and do not return tonight, our pathway may shrink until it ceases to exist. Then we'll be stuck here in '98. And not only that, as you followed the same pathway as me, you placed the pathway under stress, leading to pathway fracture, allowing other dimensions access to this time. Dimensions that shall remain open for as long as we are present here. God knows what entities may now be a part of this world and will only go back if we return home." Future Paul explained.

Paul contemplated the clock in his house and Josephine's revelation regarding her reflection - Jason and the letter. He pondered the gaming hall and his journey back in time to visit his mother, attributing the peculiar occurrences to Future Paul and Beatrice's escapades through time.

Future Paul faced Paul.

"You. I mean, we are still marrying her, or I wouldn't still be here," Future Paul said, pointing at Beatrice.

"You are not listening," Future Paul barked at Paul.

"I am. But what about what she's saying about me, I mean us, murdering Josephine?" Paul responded.

Future Paul chuckled.

"It's not true! Oh my goodness! She's got into you guys' heads. This woman is sick! Even if you asked her her name, you'd have to ask twice to make sur…" Paul began, his words simmering into silence, his face becoming thoughtful.

The playground fell silent, all eyes upon Future Paul.

"Your name..." Future Paul said to Beatrice whilst clicking his fingers.

"What?" Beatrice responded.

Future Paul pointed at his wife.

"Your name. I remember now. You weren't born Beatrice; you began using your middle name in your twenties. You were Alicia when we were young. How could I have forgotten?" Future Paul said.

Future Paul faced Paul.

"You…I mean, we were looking out for uh Beatrice, but instaaa…" Future Paul said, beginning to slur, gripping his stomach, keeling over - unable to finish his sentence.

Suddenly, Beatrice released Josephine and began walking backwards clumsily, patting her belly before she knelt over and wrapped her arms around her midriff.

Paul stepped away from Future Paul, and Josephine stepped further away from Beatrice, both of whom had begun to groan.

"Do..o..o.. on't believe him," Beatrice stammered.

Josephine and Paul stepped even further away from the pair of them, concerned about their behaviour.

"Look out for Aliciaaa!" Future Paul shouted, becoming transparent. A bright light shone around him and Beatrice, forcing Josephine and Paul to cover their eyes from the intense glare.

The light engulfed and drew Beatrice and Future Paul into it until they had disappeared, leaving Josephine and Paul alone in the park.

A minute passed, and Paul and Josephine stood in silence, staring at the point of Paul and Beatrice's departure.

Josephine shook her head slowly, then turned to Paul.

"Promise me you're not going to..." Josephine said, gesturing with a stabbing motion in the air.

Paul didn't acknowledge her.

"Paul!" Josephine said.

"Can this night get any madder? " Paul questioned.

"Paul. If you are planning on murdering me, so help me, God, boy. " Josephine stated.

Paul laughed.

"It doesn't work like that; if I was gonna murk you, I wouldn't tell you, would I?" Paul responded with a wink.

Josephine appeared shocked.

"So you are," Josephine said.

Paul kissed his teeth.

"Can we just go?" Paul said, sounding frustrated.

Paul offered Josephine a handshake.

"Friends," Paul said.

Josephine looked at Paul's outstretched hand, released a sigh, and reached out to shake it. But just as she was about to do so, Paul pulled his hand back, brushing over the top of his head.

"Sike!" Paul shouted.

Josephine turned her open hand into a fist and punched his shoulder. Paul began to laugh.

"Idiot!" Josephine responded.

"Come, let's go before I get a little crazy," Paul said, forcing a twitching eye and a nervous tic. Josephine pushed him in the back as they walked towards the park's exit.

Their route to the main road was unremarkable. They passed maisonettes and small blocks of flats on either side of the road till it delivered them to the top of the Harrow Rd, a lively and vibrant mini-high street that stretched to and beyond Harlesden, where they were headed.

The Harrow Road was predominantly occupied by young people out and about enjoying the final weekend of the summer.

A pub blared pop music, and a few doors down, a Caribbean restaurant/bar played Soca and Bashment - some elderly gentlemen were seated outside it in a group, slamming dominoes and drinking rum.

A few older teenagers loitered on the corners looking shifty.

Off-licences experienced a steady stream of people arriving on foot and pulling up in cars blaring 'House and Garage' music, stocking up on alcohol and cigarettes, fuelling a night just beginning or ones they were reluctant to see end.

Josephine and Paul ambled along, scanning and staring, searching for any other peculiar occurrences.

"Now they've gone back, I hope that's the end of the weird stuff," Paul said.

"That makes two of us,

From their left, across the street, someone called out, "Oi!"

They were both startled and turned towards the voice. It was Paul's taxi driver from earlier. He was parked up on the opposite side of the road.

He beckoned them over.

Paul and Josephine remained motionless.

"Come 'ere, I need to talk to you." the taxi driver said.

Josephine and Paul whispered between themselves.

"What should we do?"

"I don't have the fare; might have to duck him," Paul said.

"Come! I just want to ask your dad something." The taxi driver assured.

Josephine looked to Paul for their next course of action.

"Wait here for me," Paul said to Josephine.

"No, we go together," Josephine said.

"Nah, it's cool, look how much people are out here, nothing ain't happening, truss," Paul assured.

Paul crossed the road and approached the taxi driver's window.

"Where's your dad?" the taxi driver asked.

"He's gone somewhere with my mum," Paul replied.

The taxi driver gazed at a spot on the windscreen, and Paul observed the glaring red digital numbers on the taxi driver's dashboard, which displayed a fare Paul could not afford to pay.

"Right, I'm gonna have to hang on to this until I speak to him - the issue is I can't get the screen lock off. Do you know how?" The taxi driver asked, holding the iPhone.

"Nah, my dad doesn't allow me to touch his stuff," Paul responded.

The taxi driver fell silent. Then, he placed the phone down on the passenger seat and produced an old receipt and pen from his jacket.

He wrote down his telephone number.

"Here, that's my number. When you get home, you give it to your old man, tell him to give me a ding. I have questions about the device, like why it has an Apple Macintosh logo on the back and how it works.

I don't think this is a gaming device; look at those symbols at the top of the screen. Looks more like a phone to me," the taxi driver said, holding the receipt with the number on it for Paul to take.

Paul took it and stuffed it in his back pocket.

"You tell him I couldn't give a monkey's about the fare, as long as I get a proper go on this." The taxi driver said, mesmerised by the handset, slipping it in and out of his palms, brushing the screen with his thumb, and pulling the unlock button back and forth.

"Look, it's touch screen and all sorts, and look, this image comes up when you leave it for a while. Proper, crystal clear—it's like something out of the future," the taxi driver said.

Paul stood straight and sighed.

"It would be nice to have some insider knowledge of this before I start my internship with Apple Macintosh. Please make sure he dings me, will ya?" the taxi driver pleaded.

"Will do," Paul said.

"My name's Clive Sinclair, by the way." The taxi driver informed Paul.

Clive broke eye contact and went back to playing with the phone. Paul turned and navigated through traffic across the road back to Josephine.

"What did he say?" Josephine asked.

"Nothing much. Come, let's walk and talk," Paul suggested.

They began to walk towards Kensal Rise, a small town situated between Paddington and their final destination, Harlesden.

"Paul gave him a phone from the future to hold until we gave him money - so we could come after you. The man loves computers and all that, so he's asking me to tell my dad to ring him so they can talk about the phone," Paul said.

"Dad?" Josephine questioned.

"Yeah, Paul told him we were father and son."

"Why?" Josephine asked.

"Paul was acting mad with me, so he told him I was his son," Paul responded.

"Anyway, he wants me to tell Paul to call him so he can get into the phone."Paul continued.

"Hmmm. I wonder why the phone didn't go back as well?" Josephine questioned.

"Don't know," Paul said with a shrug.

Josephine suddenly grabbed Paul, stopping him in his tracks.

"That could cause serious issues, you know," Josephine stated.

"What you on about?" Paul replied.

"Think back to the future - cause and effect," Josephine said.

"What if that phone staying here creates a serious societal issue?" She continued.

"Don't be stupid. How can a phone cause soc. Soc. Socity issues? Or whatever you said, it's just a phone."

"But it's not just a phone. It's a high-tech phone. Think about it. Look at how the man was willing to risk his fare just to have time on it. What if he gets it to a major company, and they start mass producing it, and those phones become super addictive like drugs? What if, like him, people couldn't stop looking at them, unable to put them down - had them out at the dinner table, on the bus, the train - constantly on them like he was? What if people started to live on the phone instead of in reality? I've studied addiction; it's a slippery slope." Josephine reasoned.

Paul laughed.

"It's not funny; we should destroy it," Josephine suggested.

"You must be going mad, I don't understand a word you're saying, and to keep it real - I don't care about any of this. I want this night to be over. I ain't chasing no taxi man to get no phone - no way! Right now. I'm going to the park. And as soon as daylight licks, I'm going home - and you and me ain't never gonna chat 'bout this night again - We got lost on the way to the party and went straight back, that's what we're telling everyone - you get me." Paul said.

"That's a no then?" Josephine said.

Paul kissed his teeth.

✳✳✳✳✳

The further they walked down the Harrow Rd, the quieter it became. The vibrant establishments began to dwindle on both sides of the street, making way for businesses that had closed during regular operating hours.

It became so quiet that you wouldn't have thought they were on the same stretch of road.

The pair stopped at a crossing—with Kensal Rise to their right, and Kensal Green ahead. Vehicles trickled by, back and forth in a criss-cross.

"What was her name again?" Paul asked.

"Who?"

"Beatrice. I mean her other name?" Paul responded.

"Oh. Alicia."

"That's it. I'm not gonna lie. Beatrice looked kinda buff, and a little like -"

"Oh my God! Your pocket's glowing," Josephine shouted, pointing at Paul's jeans pocket. Paul glanced downwards at the rectangular shape radiating light through the fabric of his trousers; they both regarded the sight with wonder.

Paul looked to where Josephine had placed her own.

"So's yours," Paul said, pointing.

They both fixed their gaze upon their travel cards pulsating with light.

"Get it out then," Josephine said.

Paul felt apprehensive.

"You first," Paul replied, standing with his arms out, hovering, as if he were playing a game of 'stick in the mud'.

"What if it says something weird?" Paul questioned.

They both paused in thought, staring at each other.

"I don't think we have a choice. Like Jason said, I think this has to play out for us to complete this and get home," Josephine murmured.

Paul looked skyward, then placed his hand in his pocket, anticipating heat, a tingling sensation, or any other reaction from the card—but there was nothing.

He gripped the card between his fingers, withdrew it, then turned it over and began reading.

Josephine took a tentative step towards him.

"Well?" Josephine asked.

Paul looked up.

"It says Kensal Rise - Now…"

They both looked to their right towards Kensal Rise's direction, a direction they had not intended on going.

The road going up there was eerily quiet, almost desolate.

Kensal Rise and Kensal Green were two parts of a small town situated between Paddington and Harlesden. It contained two railway stations, Kensal Green train station (situated on Harrow Road up ahead of them) and Kensal Rise train station (which was within Kensal Rise to their right).

Josephine puffed out her cheeks, then withdrew her card and read it.

Paul observed her in anticipation.

She paused, then glanced up at him.

"Well?" Paul asked.

She looked perplexed.

"Yo, what is it!" Paul questioned.

"Kensal Green - Now." Josephine replied.

Paul frowned.

"But that's down there.. Nah man, we're getting split," Paul said, pointing up the road.

"Looks like it," Josephine replied.

Paul's eyes danced in their sockets, his brain pushing and pulling thoughts around his head.

"We don't have to - no one's forcing us," Paul reasoned.

"That's exactly what's happening - we're being forced by someone powerful. Someone taking pleasure in torturing us tonight." Josephine said.

"What? Well, who do you think that is?" Paul questioned.

Josephine pointed at the church they were standing in front of. Paul turned, looked at it and turned back.

"No way." Paul responded.

Josephine nodded.

Paul shook his head from side to side.

"Yes way. He took my dad. Then our house and turned my brother into a monster. I don't care what anybody says; he hates me. Look at what we've been through today." Josephine said.

Paul shook his head slowly.

"It's not like tha -" Paul began.

"You can't tell me what anything is like! You haven't lived my life!" Josephine barked, stepping back from Paul.

"Look at your own situation. No dad. Poor. Living in the worst place in London. You and your friends stand around hoping things will change - It won't - He won't let it happen. People like us aren't favoured by him," Josephine continued.

"What're you on about! You saw my future self, wealthy and successful; things can change with God's grace." Paul responded.

"What are you talking about! Can't you see that we're being manipulated for his amusement?" Josephine questioned.

Paul shook his head.

"I don't believe that. Pastor Tion always says that life is a journey, guided by the decisions we make and the challenges we overcome. God gave us life and free will with it. If we make the right decisions,

we will be fine tonight, we just have to have faith."
Paul responded.

Josephine regarded Paul through a scowl, as if he
had cursed her mother. Then her expression became
stern, her gaze cruel and piercing. Tears streamed
down both her cheeks, her lips pulled back, exposing
her angry gums and grinding teeth.

"Your just repeating irrelevant stuff from a fantasy
book. How could you believe any of that after what's
happened to us? Look. Have you ever watched a
person become a drug addict?" Josephine questioned.

Paul looked at her blankly - the whites of her eyes
so wide they looked like they would consume her
face.

"Have you? A human transformed into a... a...
fiend.. Almost soulless, like those people from the
gaming hall, but instead of games, it's a rock formed
from God's earth. I have a diary filled with them at
home. What kind of God would allow that? Ha!"
Josephine growled.

Paul remained silent, searching for words and
beginning to feel a little scared of the ones coming
out of Josephine's mouth. *Blasphemy* came to mind.

"Exactly…So please don't talk to me about faith! I
have no faith. I don't believe in anything anymore!"
Josephine said through gritted teeth.

She then threw her travel card to the floor, turned,
and began crossing the road, walking towards Kensal
Green.

Paul stood by, watching her leave.

"Yo! Take that back!.. Josephine! Joesphine!!
You-take-that-back-now!!!" Paul shouted.

She didn't.

Paul released a deep sigh and looked down at her travel card on the floor, its glow gradually diminishing.

He bent down and retrieved it.

He scrutinised it. It had faded to no more than a black rectangle with nothing to report.

He contemplated going after her. He even started walking but stopped. Nothing felt right about it—the compulsion to get to the destination on his travel card was far greater.

He felt wetness on his hand and realised they were his tears; he was crying for Josephine, over the dreadful emotions she was experiencing and the cruel words she had uttered.

Paul had attended church and Sunday school from the age of four until the age of fourteen, and although he would not profess to be the most knowledgeable believer, he held firm beliefs and faith in the Almighty.

There existed an abundance of love within the walls of his church, and many flawed, selfless, emotionally broken people from his local area who possessed little financial worth, yet still found something to give to those less fortunate than themselves. Paul had witnessed too many men and women who had fallen by the wayside of life, whom the world would have deemed finished, yet had found their way to the church and, through dedication and ultimately their belief in God, had reformed and now were of value to themselves and the world once more.

Paul had witnessed numerous instances of warmth, love, kindness and selflessness to doubt whether the people surrounding him in those four walls were adhering to a fallacy.

The Scriptures were their script; their positive actions stemmed from their belief in God and the teachings of the Bible.

Josephine was correct. She had observed the gradual progression of a drug addict, yet she was not privy to the addicts who had found their way back into the flock and once more thrived.

Paul wiped his face, pocketed Josephine's travel card, and then looked at his own, gleaming like a star over lightless waters.

I have to finish this - Paul contemplated. *She has her path, and I have mine. May God be with both of us.*

With that, Paul set off for Kensal Rise train station, his heart heavy, hoping to at last reach home.

✳ ✳ ✳ ✳ ✳

"Oh dear. What do the pages say about this?" Hemsut asked.

"Very unexpected."

The two Moirai observe silence.

"So much damage - she comes and goes," Hemsut said.

"Hmm, she has endured a lot. That's why I wanted to bind them - I know Paul can steer her back towards the path," Istustaya said.

"Well, he-who-shall-not-be-named has thrown a curve ball here - separated them when she needed company the most."

168

Istustaya looked off into the heavens - a blue sky blanketed with countless stars - resting amidst plump, cotton-white clouds poised in flawless radiance.

"Well...The night isn't over yet. There is still time." She murmured.

*****

Kensal Green cemetery flanked Josephine's left, its walls tall and menacing—built in a style of stone craftsmanship the New World had long forgotten—raised and quilted in appearance, chipped and chiselled without style or finesse—robust.

Designed to retain the deceased and exclude the living, when the gates close for the day.

It is dark and desolate on this stretch of the Harrow Road - hardly any people or cars travelling.

At intervals along the cemetery's stone wall, the stone gives way to steel grates that afford passing people a glimpse into its eternal residents' residences.

Josephine kept her head straight as she passed the first grate, but by the second, she noticed someone matching her stride on the opposite side of the wall; upon reaching the third grate, Josephine slowed to a standstill and looked directly at the figure standing amongst the gravestones and tombs cloaked in darkness, wearing the night as cover.

The individual stared at her.

Then, they commenced walking towards her, and Josephine's knees nearly gave way. Her heart began to race.

"What is this now..." Josephine whispered.

She turned to flee, but ahead, another person approached, advancing with purpose.

She then glanced to her right across the road, turned, and realised she was being surrounded from all sides.

As they neared, the pursuers on the street became clearer—they were the Stonebridge boys from earlier, but something seemed off about them. They were not yelling or shouting threats; they were subdued.

Josephine peered through the grate once more, grabbed hold of two of the railings, and attempted to climb on top of the wall, but the individual within the cemetery was now up close and staring into her eyes through the grate.

It was Atë, the woman from the arcade, and she was no longer donning a human guise.

Josephine recoiled in fear; her hands clasped over her mouth.

Atë's skin is pale, her lips black, and her eyes the colour of gold mixed with shimmering glitter. They are alluring, pulling Josephine into them.

Josephine's hands fell from her mouth, down by her side - limp. She is frozen, ensnared within herself. She desires to escape, yet is paused by Atë's captivating gaze.

Josephine hears Atë's voice without words.

I am of Olympus. No man child maketh mischief with me. I heard your words. You and I are alike. Your father has cast you out from his flock and sent you adrift. Let us make the world of man pay together.

✳✳✳✳✳

Hemsut dangles Josephine's string between the open blades of her scissors.

"This is such a shame. You gave it your best, sister," Hemsut said of Istustaya's efforts.

"Wait..." Istustaya responded.

"Wait?"

Istustaya shook her head.

"She isn't going off her free will. She is being coerced by Atë, who doesn't even belong in this dimension," Istustaya said.

"It doesn't matter. She wouldn't be able to be coerced if there wasn't sizeable susceptibility; you heard what she said to Paul," Hemsut argued.

"She didn't mean it. The night has frayed her nerves. Humans are fragile creatures. Look. If he-who-shall-not-be-named can directly influence through Atë, then I am free to respond. I shall not lose this one. I have a feeling it's far too important."

With that, Istustaya set to work.

✳✳✳✳✳

Paul lurched towards Kensal Rise train station. At intervals, he walked backwards, hoping Josephine had had a change of heart and was rushing towards him like an epic ending to one of those romance films his mother detested—but instead, there were only the occasional people walking by in the distance.

Two hundred metres until he reached the train station, and he hoped that would be the final part of his night of lunacy.

171

Home. That was all he desired now - to return to his mother and brother, in familiar surroundings where things were unremarkable.

He looked forward to his mother standing listening to the radio, ironing both his and his brother's church shirts and trousers whilst darting in and out of the kitchen to tend to their Sunday dinner, shouting up the staircase for Paul to hurry up and get his younger brother ready for Pastor Tion's marathon church service, which endured for what seemed an eternity.

Paul smiled at the thought.

*****

"Yo, slow down! Ain't that Josephine?" Fabian said, pointing out of the car's windscreen up ahead.

Xavier's brother slowed the car.

"Yeah, What's she doing with them guys?"

"Forget that, where's P?"

"That doesn't look right."

Xavier's brother slowed the car further until it crawled. They mounted the kerb and stopped. The boys nearing Josephine peered into the headlights, their eyes reflecting the glare like cats.

All fell silent within the vehicle, Paul's friends trying to fathom the scene before them.

"Yo, I ain't no expert on anything, yeah, but man's eyes ain't supposed to be doing that."

Xavier's brother pulled a facial expression that suggested his logic was being challenged.

One of the boys snarled at them, then advanced towards Josephine. Xavier's brother pressed the accelerator, and in an instant, the vehicle surged towards the Stonebridge boys, forcing them to leap aside and scatter in all directions to evade collision. Xavier's brother parked the vehicle directly alongside Josephine.

"Get her in the car!" Xavier's brother bellowed.

Fabian opened the rear door, sprang out, wrapped his arms around Josephine's waist, and tumbled back into the vehicle. By this time, the Stonebridge boys had regrouped and were running towards them.

Atë floated up and over the cemetery wall, then swooped down upon the vehicle.

Paul's friends heard a loud bang on top of the car's roof. The metal groaned under her weight.

Xavier's brother sped away with Josephine and Fabian, partially in and out of the car. Josephine was slumped between Fabian's legs, the car door swinging, trying to close.

"What the hell!" Slim shouted from the back seat, his arms under Fabian's armpits, trying to keep him from being thrown out of the car.

"Rah! Dem man are catching up!" Xavier said from the front passenger seat, looking in the wing mirror at the four boys chasing them.

Atë clung to the sides of the roof and peered into the car. Her eyes blazed, her black lips pulled back over black teeth and gums.

Fabian and Slim began to scream and shout at her terrifying appearance. She hissed and reached in, attempting to seize Josephine. Fabian started kicking frantically, attempting to stop her.

Josephine began to regain consciousness, mumbling incoherently.

Xavier's brother glanced back at the commotion behind him and applied the brakes, propelling everyone in the car forward and launching Atë fifty metres ahead.

Two loud bangs sounded from beneath the car. The aroma of the hot engine, scorched brakes and tyres filled the vehicle.

Xavier's brother attempted to accelerate again, only to hear the sound of metal rims scraping against the road.

Xavier's brother closed his eyes and struck the steering wheel and dashboard repeatedly with his palm.

"Flats!" Xavier's brother shouted!

"Pull her in!" Slim screamed at Fabian, his chest pumping.

Fabian pulled Josephine inside and slammed the door.

Xavier glanced back; the Stonebridge boys were upon them, kicking, pushing and pulling the car. One of the boys was at the rear window, whilst the other three were on either side of the car, attempting to break in.

The passenger windows began to crack, then they shattered.

Josephine was trapped in the middle seat, squeezed between Slim and Fabian, who were both leaning against her and kicking at the hands of the boys attempting to pull Josephine out.

Within the vehicle, pandemonium reigns, with everyone shouting and screaming.

The rear window begins to shatter under the boys' assault.

The boy on Slim's side seized Slim's leg and was trying to pull him through the windowless frame. Xavier's brother turned and grasped Slim to prevent him from being dragged out.

Atë finally gathered herself and soared ten metres in the air. Her dress had amassed mass, swirling like black smoke around her. Her eyes shone golden, and she plummeted down upon the car, tearing the roof clean off.

The Stonebridge boys were sent hurtling four hundred metres up the road.

Xavier, Fabian, Xavier's brother and Slim stared upwards into the open air, rendered speechless as metal shards and broken glass from the car trailed behind Atë into the night sky.

She dropped the roof upon the Stonebridge boys.

"Useless humans," Atë shrieked.

She redirected her focus back to the car.

No man child maketh mischief with me, she said. Everyone raised their hands to their ears, Atë's words as loud as church bells in their heads. They collapsed around the car, dazed.

Josephine shot up, turned, and looked skyward at Atë hovering, staring down at her, preparing to swoop.

But before she did so, the clouds began to sparkle, crackling and snapping with electricity. Internally illuminated like Chinese lanterns floating above.

A powerful light emanates from behind Josephine, compelling her to turn from Atë to look at the source.

Lightning scrambled across the skies, clinging to every contour of the clouds—then came a rumble that sounded as if the world was on the verge of fracturing and splitting.

Zeus's sentries appear in the sky, adorned in their golden armour, with spears and shields, hurtling towards Atë.

Atë shrieked and transformed into a jet-black eagle, shooting off with Zeus's sentries in pursuit, their armour sparkling like shooting stars across the nocturnal sky. Within seconds, it was as if they had never been there.

Silence reigns.

Josephine and Paul's friends exited the car.

They gathered around the Stonebridge boys who lay beneath the car's roof. They were now restored to their human form, alive but in poor condition.

"Rah, ain't that Crow and Steam from Bridge?" Slim asked.

"Yeah, it is," Fabian said.

"What the hell just happened. Who was that woman ting?" Fabian continued.

Xavier turned to Josephine.

"More importantly, where's Paul?" Xavier asked.

Everyone looked at her.

She looked bewildered.

"Yeah, where is he?" Slim asked.

She looked across all of them, her eyes wide.

"I need to complete this, or everything will stay as it is," Josephine murmured.

"What?" Xavier's brother said.

"He's gone to Kensal Rise station, and I have to get to Kensal Green," Josephine said, mumbling as she began to walk off.

"What. On the train?"

"Yeah, bu...I...I, can't explain right now,"
Josephine whispered as she began to back away from
them.

"To where, though? Trains finished hours ago!"

"Yo! You can't just go on your jays. There's weird
stuff gwaning; look at them," Fabian said, pointing at
the Stonebridge boys.

"I'll be fine," Josephine responded as she turned
and began to jog.

* * * * *

"Take that Atë "Hemsut said.

"Told you Zeus wouldn't tolerate this." Istustaya
added.

"Hold on. What about Paul's friends getting there
just in time?" Hemsut questioned.

"I give humans the inclinations, ideas, and feelings;
it's up to them whether they act upon them. Let's call
it an informed coincidence." Istustaya responded.

Hemsut chuckled.

"With you, there are no coincidences." Hemsut
replied.

* * * * *

Paul stood outside the entrance to Kensal Rise train
station. The station is dark except for the digital clock
above the stairs leading down to the platforms. Its red
neon numerals read 14:08.

177

Paul closed his eyes and stepped off the kerb into the station, whereupon the doors immediately slammed shut behind him.

He stood in the darkness, gazing at the clock's numbers piercing the blackness. His thoughts turned to Josephine. He wished she were there.

He closed his eyes, trying to suppress the wish and when he opened them, the clock read, "The world will see you now".

Paul proceeded towards a balcony which had two staircases at opposite ends leading down to platforms one and two.

He looked over the balcony, observing the train tracks vanishing into pitch-black darkness.

Small bulkheads were affixed to the brick platform walls. They emit an orange light to illuminate both platforms.

In the distance, two yellow lights appear, growing larger by the second.

He noticed his pocket was glowing once more. Paul buried his hand in it and extracted the ticket.

It reads "Platform 1".

He watched the approaching train for a number of seconds. He then murmured a brief prayer before descending to the platform.

He walked along the platform until midway, then stopped.

The train entered the station and came to a standstill. It was a freight train, akin to the ones that would rattle or rumble past Paul and his friends whilst they were in the park at night, daydreaming in the darkness, unaware of the manifestations they were casting beneath the stars.

Rich and Fabian particularly detested life on the estate; they consistently discussed moving to the suburbs, and their shared aspiration was fulfilled for both.

Xavier craved the intellect and maturity of his elder brother—granted, and Paul aspired to know where the freight trains went.

"It's a freight train; it goes everywhere,"

Rich's words rattled around Paul's head once more.

"But where will this take me?' Paul whispered, looking at the dirty, dust-covered train cabs.

A door opened, and a conductor emerged, a tall, slender Sikh man adorned with a white turban, with a lengthy white beard and whiskers.

His uniform is dapper, tailored to fit, and royal blue with gold stitching. He has a ticket pouch and dispenser machine strapped around his waist.

The pair looked each other over. Paul regarded him with suspicion, and given the night he had had so far, this was not without good reason.

Out of nowhere and at the top of his lungs, the man shouted, "All aboard!" Startling Paul - sending pigeons perched on the surrounding walls of the station up into the air, beating wings into the night sky.

The man clicked his heels together, smiled and winked. Paul's frown slowly faded, replaced by a smirk at the man's exaggerated mannerisms.

The conductor nodded.

"There it is. You're far too young to look so old. Please board," the conductor said.

Paul nodded and walked towards him.

The man stepped aside and held out his hand.

"I need to see your ticket before you ride the train to wherever you care."

"Oh," Paul said, pulling out the travel card and handing it to him. The man looked at it, then over the card at Paul, down again, then over at Paul; this went on for twenty seconds before he opened his pouch and shoved the travel card between other glowing tickets.

"Wow! How many people are on this?" Paul asked, examining his collection of cards.

"They rode the freight train to wherever you care earlier. It's just you and me, kid… For now."

Paul nodded and stepped aboard, and as soon as his foot crossed the threshold, the drab interior transformed and became bright and luxurious - like the steam trains of old - the carriages lit by toffee-coloured glass lights that jutted out of the walls over tables and chairs for four.

Each table had a bouquet of colourful flowers and a jug of water. Sparkling knives and forks sat beside ivory plates.

The seats were velvet and green with brown wooden frames. The carpet was a deep racing green that ran from one carriage to the next through large teak-coloured vestibule doors.

It smelled as one would imagine.

Paul had never encountered anything so beautiful; he stood surveying the carriage, his modern attire clashing with the period of the décor.

The conductor stood behind Paul, relishing Paul's delight.

"One must be seated if one is to ride the freight train to wherever you care," the conductor remarked, withdrawing a seat to Paul's right.

Paul sat, and the conductor pushed his seat in; Paul turned to say thank you, but the conductor had disappeared.

Paul looked around frantically, rotating in his chair.

Psssssssh - the loud sound of the train's brakes disengaging startled Paul.

Overhead, Paul heard a crackle and pop from the speakers above, coming to life.

"Welcome to your 14:08 train to your destiny; my name is Kisamata—your driver, and carer for the journey. Now that's out of the way, do you want to see if she's there? But be warned. Before you make that decision, if you ask to stop and she isn't, you will have to get off and continue home on foot."

The train commenced its movement.

Paul searched for a microphone to respond.

"Talk into the air; I can hear you," Kisamata announced.

"Can you say that again? I don't get it." Paul responded.

"You can stop this train at the next station to see if Josephine turns up, but if she isn't there, you will have to continue the journey on foot," Kisamata said.

Paul sat pensively, Josephine's final words reverberating in his mind.

Paul was fatigued mentally, spiritually and physically. The prospect of taking a chance on Josephine being at Kensal Green—with her more than likely not—resulting in him having to get off the comfortable, luxurious train and walk home with whatever the night had left for him wasn't appealing, to say the least.

"Well?" Kisamata announced.

Paul gazed out of the window at the darkness pressed against the glass.

"Come now. We don't have all night?" Kisamata added.

If he did not take the opportunity and see whether she was there, she would have to continue on foot, confronting any obstacles ahead alone. Paul puffed out his cheeks and closed his eyes.

"Well.."

"Errr. Okay, stop," Paul said.

"Good," Kisamata said.

"I mean, she did say some stuff that…That ain't cool, but I know she didn't mean it; she was angry. Trust me. She has a kind heart." Paul replied.

"Young man, you don't need to explain. In life, we have to make tough choices on whether to do the right or wrong things. Each of them bears consequences."

Paul didn't like the word "consequence." For him, a consequence has always carried a negative slant. In his short life, he had yet encountered anyone who had experienced positive consequences for their actions.

"So if she isn't there, you'll leave me at the station," Paul wanted to confirm.

"Precisely," Kisamata replied.

Paul gazed out of the window. He observed Kensal Green drawing closer.

He began to doubt his decision. What reason did he have to believe Josephine would be there? He had none, but he yearned for and needed her to be there.

Aside from his mother and Pastor Tion, Paul had never encountered anyone else who instilled hope in him as Josephine did.

She was prim and proper, and she embodied a world beyond his horizon—she had lived in his desired destination.

"We're approaching Kensal Green. This is your last chance, Paul. Do we persist or pause?" Kisamata questioned.

Paul observed the station as it grew in size with its approach.

"Paul.." Kisamata said.

"Okay. Stop,"

"So be it." Kisamata responded.

Paul rose and grasped the handrail above, gazing out of the window.

They entered the station, and he could not see anyone there. The train brakes began to hiss, the sound of them bringing the train to a jerky stop.

Paul approached the doors, which opened. He stood in the doorway, glanced left and then right along the platform.

Empty.

"I'm sorry, young man, this is where our journey must end, I'm afraid."

Paul turned around to find Kisamata standing behind him.

"You took a chance, that's good. Always take a chance; you never know what could happen. You are most selfless and noble, I admire that. Regrettably, you were unfortunate on this occasion." Kisamata stated.

"Bu-" Paul began.

"Sorry, but you'll have to disembark," Kisamata said, cutting in.

"Bu-" Paul tried again.

"Good luck and mind the gap, young man. Our business here is over."

"Please.." Paul whispered.

Kisamata sighed.

"Don't make this harder than it has to be," Kisamata mumbled.

"Come on, man. How can you do this?" Paul protested.

Kisamata stepped around Paul onto the platform.

"You made a choice. People live and die on them every day. Please." Kisamata said, his arm outstretched, offering Paul the platform.

Paul shook his head and stepped off. Kisamata stepped back on the train.

He clicked his heels together and gave Paul a salute.

"Khuśakisamatī". Kisamata said.

"What?" Paul responded.

"Good luck," Kisamata replied.

With that, the doors shut, and Kisamata turned his back and began walking down the train's gangway.

The train's interior began to lose its radiance and became dark. Paul looked up the platform and focused on the steps leading up to the street—he was once again going out to.

He glanced back at the train, now no more than a dirty freight again.

Paul commenced walking towards the platform staircase, observing the train still docked. The red tail and side lights illuminated, and the train started to move. Paul took a deep breath.

As he gazed up at the landing above the stairs, he saw something dart across the train station foyer towards the staircase leading down to him.

He paused, waiting for the monster's arrival, but when the creature rounded the corner, it was no creature at all; it was Josephine. His eyes widened.

Before his brain could register, he was shouting.

"Hurry!" Paul screamed, waving her over.

He turned towards the train which had barely left the station and was moving at a snail's pace.

When he turned back, Josephine was on the platform, sprinting towards him. Paul began to jog—like relay runners do, looking back at their team-mates waiting for the baton.

"Come on!" He shouted towards her.

When she caught up, he seized her arm, and the pair started sprinting down the platform.

"Ay! She's here!" Paul screamed, waving his free hand frantically at the back of the train.

"Ayyy! She came! She came!" Paul shouted.

They were running out of platform, and the train was beginning to gather speed.

When they reached the end of the platform, Paul stopped and turned to Josephine, gasping for breath.

"We gotta get on the track!"

"No-ho-ho ..way," Josephine replied.

"If we don't get on that train, I don't know how this will end." Paul declared.

Josephine groaned.

"We can do it," Paul said.

Josephine peered down at the track beneath the platform, then sat on her bottom and descended onto it.

"Come on then, let's go home," Josephine said.

With that, Paul leapt down, and the pair started running, chasing the train - its tail lights bleeding neon red into the darkness. The rear door of the train swung open, leaving a rectangle of white light in its place.

At full pace now, Paul and Josephine are sprinting once more.

Paul gets within touching distance of the handrail people would use to descend from the open door onto three small steps at the train's rear.

He gritted his teeth, injected the last of his energy, and grasped the bar, hauling himself onto the steps.

He looked back, and Josephine was beginning to slow down.

"Joe! Come on, man!" Paul shouted.

She was fading badly. Paul walked into the carriage and began to scream.

"Stop the train! She's here! She came! Stop this train now!" Paul shouted whilst staring back at Josephine, who had now stopped running and was bent over, trying to catch her breath.

Paul looked around, for what - he knew not. Then he glanced upwards and saw a large red lever, which he reached up and pulled.

Beneath the train, the brakes began to squeal until the train came to a halt.

Paul turned back to the door, and Josephine - detailed by her cream cardigan in the distance.

"Come on!" Paul screamed out, worried the train might get going again.

Josephine began to jog.

As Josephine reached the steps, she gazed up at Paul.

"What're you waiting for?" Paul said to her.

"My ticket, where is it?" Josephine screamed.

Paul looked perplexed.

"Why?"

"I told you earlier that I don't bunk cabs, that includes trains! Can't ride if I haven't got a ticket."

"Oh, my days!" Paul said, shaking his head simultaneously, rummaging around for her ticket in his jeans pocket.

He withdrew it and offered it to her.

"You picked it up?" Josephine said.

"Course. Thought you'd need it."

"How'd you know I was going to come?"

"I just did," Paul said with a shrug.

Josephine gazed past him.

"I'm sorry about what I said earlier."

"It's all right. Don't worry about it." Paul responded.

Josephine nodded, then extended her hand.

"Friends," Josephine said.

They both paused, staring at each other. Paul broke eye contact, looked down at her hand, and gave her the travel card.

"Come, let's find Kisamata," Paul said.

She held the travel card, turning it over until it regained its colour - starting from the edges inwards, sparkling gold. She looked up at Paul and smiled.

"The world will see you now," Josephine said, reading aloud.

Paul stood in the doorway, beaming down at her. She looked up at the boy who could become a man her father would approve of.

She grasped the handrails, raised her leg, and brought it down onto the first step. As soon as her foot touched it, a bright white light consumed the vessel, so bright that neither of them could see their hand in front of their faces.

The pair cried out each other's names; she hurried up the stairs towards Paul - both dazzled - reaching for one another in the light; they clung tightly to each other and fell down onto the train floor, with Josephine on top of Paul between his legs.

The light abruptly ceased, and they opened their eyes. The train was grand once more - beautiful and luxurious - moving with a smooth chug.

The pair regarded one another, their faces close enough to kiss; Paul grinned, and Josephine grimaced and leapt up, quickly getting to her feet.

"Errr!" Josephine exclaimed.

Paul began to laugh, rolling about like a de-winged fly; Josephine looked down upon him.

"You're not funny, boy, your - " Josephine began, unable to finish her sentence. The sight of the train and its magnificence was breathtaking.

She twirled on her heels and then stopped and gazed at the windows—radiant daylight streaming in, drenching the train in its golden glare.

She approached the window and peered out.

"Paul.." Josephine murmured.

"Yeah."

"Come see this." Josephine continued.

"I've seen him do it already," Paul said of the changing interior.

Paul stood up and walked over to Josephine, both rendered speechless.

They were elevated upon a viaduct; it was daylight outside, and the sun was high above.

Lush evergreens flanked them, and beyond the trees stood mighty, snow-capped mountains. Red, blue and yellow chalets speckled the crayon-green hills and valleys below.

The train sliced through white steam billowing from the front.

They stood in silence, observing the world in its splendour.

"Amazing isn't it," Kisamata said, standing behind them.

Josephine turned around, and upon seeing Kisamata, she retreated towards Paul.

Paul turned and looked at him.

"A mere speck of beauty, sewn into a world filled with delights…" Kisamata said as he approached them.

"A shame some will never see half - those are the Alps, by the way," Kisamata stated, gesturing towards the window.

Paul looked over his shoulder at Josephine and gently slid his fingers under hers to ease her grip on his arm.

"He's a good guy. I met him earlier." Paul said.

"Is it," Josephine responded.

"Trust me."

The train began to come down off the viaduct smoothly into a valley. It was now surrounded by hills of lush green grass, bushes and trees. A small river ran beside it.

The sky above was blue with tufts of white, fluffy, cotton-like clouds.

Kisamata gestured towards the table and chairs situated beneath the window.

"If you would?" Kisamata requested.

The pair sat facing one another, peering out of the window.

"The valley of ten peaks - Canada," Kisamata announced, referring to their current location.

Upon the mention of Canada, the pair exchanged glances, then looked up at Kisamata, who responded with a smile.

"You appear concerned - Please do not worry; I will get you home," Kisamata reassured.

"No. No..Please take your time. This is amazing." Josephine said.

"As I said to Paul earlier, this is the train to wherever you care. Each of you may request a visit to one location - from any time period before our final destination." Kisamata explained.

The pair looked at one another, their mouths agape and their eyes wide with astonishment.

"Anywhere?" Paul said.

"Anytime?" Josephine added.

"One location each?" Paul continued.

"Yes! Yes! And yes! The sole caveat is - you cannot disembark."

Paul rose from his seat and began to pace in contemplation, trying to determine where he had always yearned to visit.

Josephine gazed out of the window without reaction; Kisamata looked down upon her.

They passed a waterfall. Josephine watched the water cascade off the cliff, forming a white froth below.

She glimpsed Kisamata's reflection in the window shimmering.

She turned to him.

"You know, don't you?" Josephine questioned.

He stared at her for several seconds, then gave her a nod.

"Will he be there?" Josephine asked.

Kisamata smiled.

"I'll try my best," Kisamata replied.

With his words, the train made a sharp turn into a dazzling white light, forcing Paul and Josephine to shield their eyes.

When the light subsided, the land was rich with red and brown mud. Green palm trees and termite mounds protruded from it. Vibrant red, purple and yellow flowers and plants were scattered throughout.

Ghanaian children ran alongside the train, waving and slapping the train's exterior.

Josephine rose from her seat looking out the window, gazing at the children's beautiful brown faces—their teeth were dazzlingly white, their eyes wide and gleaming.

Paul stood, staring out on the other side of the window.

"The Accra to Tema Rail," Kisamata stated.

"Rah. We're in Africa?" Paul said.

"Nineteen seventy-five - Accra - Ghana, to be precise. The children have just finished school." Kisamata elaborated.

"Oh…" Paul said, looking at Kisamata and then over at Josephine, who was looking from face to face at the children as the train crawled by, chaperoned by the local boys and girls - sporting their brown uniforms.

She was glued to them, switching focus quickly. Then a hand came up out of the gaggle and planted itself onto the window, and Josephine looked out at the owner's face—a teenager, taller than the rest and slight.

He was different - he looked upon her as if he knew her.

The train slowed to a stop, and while the rest of the children were bouncing around in excitement, the boy remained still, staring at Josephine, his palm firmly on the window.

Josephine raised her hand and met his—she burst into tears, and the teenager gave her a warm smile.

He raised his other hand and pressed his forehead against the glass.

Paul withdrew to Kisamata to ask questions.

The teenager outside commenced speaking in Twi.

"Her dad?" Paul questioned Kisamata.

Kisamata nodded.

Ten minutes passed, and Kisamata spoke.

"Five minutes remaining," Kisamata declared.

Josephine glanced over her shoulder at Kisamata, nodded in agreement, and persisted in conversing.

Five minutes elapsed.

"Time." Kisamata said.

The train's brakes disengaged with a hiss, and the train began to crawl.

"Say your goodbyes."

Josephine's dad began walking with the train, one palm planted on the window, the other hand blowing kisses. Josephine kissed the glass. His walk became a jog as the train gathered pace; his jog now a sprint, and then the dazzling light came and Ghana vanished.

Josephine remained transfixed for several seconds, then seated herself, gazing out the window at a picturesque, evergreen-encircled lake, glistening in the sunlight.

Paul turned to address Kisamata, but he had vanished.

Paul stared at Josephine, seeking words to say. He eventually walked over and sat facing her.

"Jo-" Paul began before being interrupted.

"He's happy and he isn't in pain." She uttered.

She turned and looked Paul directly in the eyes.

"I'm not upset; you don't have to say anything. I have what I needed." Josephine said.

Paul was relieved. She had eliminated his need to find words in a scenario reserved for adults.

"Where have you chosen?" Josephine asked, wanting to move the conversation on.

Paul paused briefly before responding.

"Home.."

"Home?" Josephine said, looking a little confused.

"Yeah. I wana get started." Paul continued.

"Started? Started on what?"

Paul's face became stern as he stared out of the window at the breathtaking scenery through which the train was traversing.

"On my future. The future, Future Paul promised," he said, nodding to himself.

He pointed out the window.

"I don't have a dad, aunts or uncles with nuff money; all I have is me and my little brother. Getting to this takes work," Paul said of the luxurious train and location.

"There's no reason why this can't be my reality if I start working hard from now," Paul continued.

"He's right!" Kisamata said through the speakers.

They both scanned the carriage for him, to no avail.

"Neither of you was blessed with the greatest beginnings - but it doesn't have to define your middle or end. You do. Choices, Paul - choices, Josephine. This world belongs to nobody but everybody at the same time."

"You asked Rich where this train goes, and he replied everywhere - he was right - you are the train - your desires and dreams the coal that glows in your pit and gives you the fuel to push harder - further - for more. You get out what you put in. You eat what you cultivate, and wear what you have sewn. We are more than mere products of our environment; our environment is a product of our diligence and dedication. Be different - radical in your thinking - break barriers. You can! You must! You will!"

The train began to gather speed. The green of the trees began to blend, blur and bleed into the brown of the bark, as did the blue and white of the sky.

The train began to hurtle like a rocket, throwing them about in their seats; both clung tightly to the arms of their chairs for dear life, closing their eyes to the light outside, a blinding white, glittering with gold and silver.

"We're on the home stretch - homeward bound. We trust you have relished the journey and depart with more than you arrived with. Rabb tuhānū āśīrvād deve." Kisamata announced.

The train rattled and shook, jostling and tugging at Paul and Josephine in their seats.

The sound of the train cutting through the atmosphere grew until a massive bang, the sound of the sound barrier being broken—the pair brought their hands to their ears to protect their hearing. Then, an abrupt stillness and silence replaced all turbulence, leaving them shrieking at the top of their lungs.

"Ahhhhhhhhhhhhhhhh!"The pair shouted.

Josephine stopped first. She opened her eyes and surveyed her surroundings before shoving Paul in the chest, who still had his eyes shut, both hands clamped over his ears and was still screaming.

Paul's eyes sprang open.

"Stop!" Josephine said, raising her voice.

Paul glanced around.

The pair were seated on the floor facing one another, surrounded by piles of newspapers. Paul and Josephine helped each other up.

They were still on a train, inching along at a slow and steady pace.

The interior was grimy and dim. A thin crack in the door admitted light intermittently as the train passed lamps along the track.

"Where are we?" Josephine asked, looking around the carriage.

"I think we're on the freight train that goes past the park, the destination on our tickets," Paul said as he began weaving between the pallets to reach the door.

"You think so," Josephine replied.

The train began to brake and came to a standstill. Paul stood upon a pallet of newspapers nearest the sliding doors.

He inserted his fingers into the door's crack and pulled rightwards. The doors opened effortlessly, and Paul stood gazing down at the park below, bathed in the beginnings of daylight.

Josephine joined him.

"We're back," Paul declared.

They assisted one another down onto the grassy embankment and walked along the slope towards the lowest section of the fence. With Paul's aid, Josephine climbed up and over.

Paul followed.

They both stood, taking in the park's stillness, enjoying the universal peace and quiet that each day began with.

Later, children and parents will occupy and cover the swings, slides and climbing frames - one last hurrah before the start of another academic year and parental respite from the six-week marathon of twenty-four-seven parenting.

Josephine looked at her wristwatch. 5.45am.

"My mum will be home in ten minutes," Josephine declared.

Paul looked across at her bedroom window overlooking where their night of wonder had all begun. Her curtains were drawn together, giving the impression that someone was at home, asleep.

Josephine inhaled deeply.

"I better get in," Josephine said.

Paul nodded.

"I gotta wait a bit," Paul replied.

They both stood in silence, averting their gaze from one another.

"I suppose this is goodbye," Josephine said, extending her hand for a handshake.

"For now," Paul replied, reaching to shake her hand, but she withdrew it and pulled it over her head.

"Sike!"

Paul smiled.

Daylight grew stronger by the second.

"Thank you," Josephine stated.

"For what?" Paul said.

"For inviting me," Josephine responded.

Paul chuckled.

"Ha. We never reached the party. There's nothing to thank me for."

"We didn't have to. Tonight meant a lot to me. Gave me something that has been missing for a long time."

Paul bowed his head to her.

"Tomorrow," Josephine said, walking backwards towards her house.

Paul watched her in retreat.

"Tomorrow?" Paul responded.

"What do you think will happen?" Josephine asked, her voice raised to accommodate the small distance she had created.

"Nothing, I hope," Paul said.

"Yeah, me too," Josephine responded.

She turned and proceeded until she reached her door, took one final glance, and entered.

Instantaneous relief washed over Paul - He needn't worry about her now. She was safe.

After a few seconds, her bedroom light turned on, and she opened her curtains and looked out upon him. At that precise moment, her mother arrived outside, exited her car, and caught Paul staring at her house. She returned his gaze for several seconds until Paul looked away. Then, she opened her door and went inside.

Josephine vanished from the window, and her bedroom light went out.

Paul had four hours to occupy himself before he could return home without arousing suspicion.

Exhausted, he proceeded to sit on the wooden park bench. Before he knew it, the emerging daylight gave way to darkness once more, and he had fallen asleep.

He awoke to being forcefully shaken by both shoulders.

"Oh, my days, P's a proper tramp!" Paul heard Fabian say.

Paul's eyelids snapped open to his friends standing over him.

Slim, Xavier and Fabian.

"What're you lot doing here? What time is it?" Paul asked.

Xavier looked at his wristwatch.

"One thirty," Xavier answered.

"One thirty!" Paul repeated, shooting up from the bench.

"In the afternoon?" Paul asked.

"Yeah. Why, what's up?" Slim said.

"My mum's gonna go nuts!" Paul replied.

His friends exchanged glances.

"Why?" Fabian asked.

"I told her I'd be back for nine," Paul said.

Fabian shook his head in disbelief.

"Bredren, we just seen your mum; she told us you came out earlier to get a shape up."

Paul looked baffled, then began feeling the sides of his head.

"Hold on, what day is it?" Paul asked.

"Saturday," Slim said.

"Saturday, what. Saturday afternoon?" Paul questioned.

"Yeah. We've just had a trim for the party tonight."

"Party to-night…" Paul murmured.

Xavier looked at Paul. Paul appeared perplexed.

"What you saying, you ain't on it no more?" Xavier asked.

Paul marched through the centre of the group, encircled them, and then retraced his steps.

"Party tonight?" Paul repeated.

Xavier looked at Fabian.

"Yeah, tonight! Bredren, whagwan with you?" Slim asked.

Paul looked from one friend to the next.

"Nothing," Paul whispered.

Fabian scrunched up his face.

"One minute," Paul said, walking away from them towards Josephine's house.

He knocked on her door and waited. After a few seconds, Josephine approached the window and opened it.

"Hello!" Josephine hollered, scanning below.

Paul stepped back from the doorway and looked up at her.

"Oh, hi," Josephine said.

"Hi," Paul responded.

"Can you.." Paul continued.

"One sec, I'm coming down," Josephine said in anticipation of his request.

Paul glanced back over his shoulder at his friends watching him.

The door opened, and Josephine emerged.

Paul scrutinised her face, and she recoiled from him, his peculiar behaviour unsettling.

"What're you doing?" Josephine asked.

Paul squinted, tilting his head to one side to look at her.

"You good, yeah?" Paul asked.

"Yeah, why wouldn't I be? Oh, you mean for the..." Josephine looked around and behind her, then got a little closer and whispered.

"Party." she said with a smile, her eyes glistening with the innocence of a child.

Paul's mouth formed an O.

"We're still going, right?" Josephine queried.

Paul stepped back from her, his eyes blinking rapidly.

"You okay?" Josephine asked.

"Yeah. I um, yeah, we're still going." Paul said.

"Good. See you later," Josephine whispered and winked before shutting the door.

Paul took a deep breath and let it out.

He left her gate, signalled to his friends that he was heading home, and began to jog back to his flat.

"Rah! She doesn't remember," Paul murmured.

On his way, Paul noticed he was being surveilled from a car. Paul slowed to a halt, astonished at whom he was staring at.

"Oh my days, it's you.." Paul said.

"What?" the man replied.

"Jason King. The letter."

Jason looked Paul up and down.

"How'd you know?" Jason asked.

"You told me."

Jason appeared lost for words.

Paul smiled.

"You don't have to be there tonight - we won't be. You ain't crazy; go live your life." Paul said.

With that, Paul continued walking, leaving Jason dumbfounded, pondering what had just occurred. This left Jason with even more questions to conquer.

Paul proceeded onwards, and Isaac from the arcade crossed his path.

Paul stopped and regarded him. Isaac looked back and slowed his pace.

"Lickle man. Why you clocking so hard?" Isaac asked.

Paul froze, seeking a response for him.

"No..nothing. Just good to see you, that's all."

Isaac looked baffled.

"What?" Isaac replied.

"Errr, just saying hi," Paul muttered and commenced walking on.

Isaac watched him depart.

What the hell? How can I be the only one who remembers? Paul pondered.

As Paul approached his block, Tanya and Alicia were standing by his stairwell.

"Hi, P, where're you-" Alicia began.

"Not now. I've got to do something." Paul said whilst passing her.

"Bu-" Alicia continued.

"Alicia, I beg you leave it. I'm not in..tresss…"

Paul stopped, turned, and grabbed Alicia's shoulders. He pulled her close.

"Oh yes, finally," Alicia said, beaming - anticipating a kiss.

Tanya placed one hand over her own mouth, snapping her fingers with her other hand, giggling.

Paul scrutinised Alicia closely and then leant back from her to gain a different perspective.

"Alicia…" Paul said.

"Yeah!"

"It's you. I mean her. Beatrice." Paul muttered before letting her go.

"Beer-tris - I mean, that's my middle name; I can be anyone you want me to be, P," Alicia said.

Paul shook his head in refusal, turned, and ascended the stairs to his flat.

"Paul! Paul! One day we'll be together, watch! All in good time!"

Paul stopped and turned to her.

"Nah, we won't." Paul said and carried on up the stairs.

"We'll see about that! I will be your Beatrice!" Alicia shouted up the stairwell.

Paul rummaged in his pocket for the keys to his front door and discovered his travel card. He removed it from the pocket and looked it. The travel card was now blank, devoid of any details, as if it had been washed a thousand times.

His front door was opened from within.

"I bet you've lost your keys again? See, now everyone's got a key to the blasted house, you know what! I ain't giving you another one; you'd better get good at timekeeping." Paul's mum ranted, flour from the fritters she was rolling, floating off and hovering, lingering in the golden sunlight.

"Mum!" Paul shouted over her - throwing his arms around her and squeezing as hard as he could. His little brother came downstairs and stood behind them. Paul extended his arm, grabbed, and pulled him into the embrace.

"Mum. Lickle bro. I've missed you all so much." Paul said.

Paul's mother's brow furrowed.

"Boy, are you crazy? You just left," Paul's mum replied.

Paul released his grip, glancing between the two.

"I know, but I love you guys. We don't say that enough in this house." Paul said.

"What the hell is wrong with you, boy?" Paul's mother responded.

Paul laughed.

"I already said you can go with your friends; there's no need for all this foolishness," Paul's mum reiterated.

Paul squeezed by his mother and entered the corridor.

"Nothing to do with that," Paul said, removing his shoes and pushing them under the stairs.

His mother shook her head and closed the front door, blocking the sunlight that had been flooding the hallway.

She opened the kitchen door to her left with her shoulder - the sound of Reggae playing on 'Unique FM' became prominent. She entered the kitchen, muttering to herself, leaving Paul and his brother.

Paul winked, and his brother smiled in return.

Paul turned and hurried upstairs.

He went to his bedroom, pushed the door open, entered, and closed the door behind him - coming face-to-face with Herbert, who was standing at the foot of Paul's bed.

Paul almost leapt to the ceiling and turned to leave, but he couldn't open the door, no matter how hard he tried.

He turned to face Herbert.

Herbert gazed at him; bars of sunlight filtering through Paul's partially open blinds cast patterns across Herbert's chest and face.

"Well?" Herbert said.

Paul did not respond.

Herbert grinned.

"No need to be afraid. I mean you no harm." Herbert continued.

Paul finally blinked.

"Well, what?" Paul responded.

"Did you find out?"

Paul considered the question.

"Find out what?"

"Where it goes?" Herbert replied - with both hands moving in the motion of train wheels turning.

Paul watched him. The feelings of fear subsided.

"Well?" Herbert continued.

Paul paused in thought.

"I think so," Paul murmured.

Herbert slowly lowered his hands to his sides. A smile spread his lips, and he gave Paul a nod.

"Good. Now you make your second chance count," Herbert said.

The pair stared at one another in silence. Paul broke eye contact and glanced towards the window for a moment. He felt discomfort radiating from the area where he would have been wounded.

"A second chance? What do you mean by that?" Paul whispered, rubbing his side and stomach.

But when Paul looked back for an explanation, Herbert was gone.

THE END

Hello, people. I hope you enjoyed reading 'SHADOWS UNDER A DIPPING SUN' as much as I did writing it. I would like to make one request of you. It would be greatly appreciated if you could leave an honest review on **Amazon** to help others discover my work.

Thank you in advance.

R.P. Falconer

~

I would like to express my gratitude to the following.

To Krystal, my lovely and supportive wife, who read through the raw manuscript and provided valuable feedback.

To my friend and trusted beta reader, Lauren, for reading the raw manuscript and also providing valuable feedback.

My sincere thanks. Love and light.

Other works by R.P. Falconer

THE SWEAT, Part 1
Compendium 3
Compendium 2
The Springs
Lilif

All of my titles are available on my Amazon page.

Please follow me on

Instagram: @RPFalconer
X: @RPFalconer
Facebook: @RPFalconer

Website
www.rpfalconer.co.uk

**Please do not forget to leave an honest review on my Amazon page.
Thanks!**